LIV

KELSIE RAE

Cover Art by Sly Fox Cover Designs
Editing by Stephanie Taylor
April 2018 Edition
Published in the United States of America

To Dory from Finding Nemo.
Thanks for reminding me to, "Just Keep Swimming!"

Blurb

Liv had her life all figured out until it was shattered by the loss of her husband. He left her a piece of him she hadn't planned on. How can she pick up the pieces when she doesn't know where to begin?

Liv:

I never imagined my life would end up this way. I thought I had everything figured out until I got the call my husband was killed in a car accident and then I realized my period was late.

- Dead Husband?: Check
- Positive Pregnancy Test?: Check
- Screwed Beyond Belief?: Double Check

Luke:

I was never supposed to see her again. That was the deal. Leave her, and my ex-best friend, behind to finally mend my broken heart and move on with life. And it was going smoothly, too. That is, until said ex-best friend dies, and and his wife, Liv, lets a secret slip at his funeral that I can't possibly ignore.

- Out of my freaking mind?: Check
- Extremely Angry Girlfriend who will kill me

when she finds out I have a new roommate?:
Check

- About to get my heart ripped in two?: Double
  Check

CHAPTER ONE

LIV

I'm pregnant.

After being married for five years to my high school sweetheart, I should be happy with the news. And I would be. *If* I wasn't staring at those two pink lines right before I head to the funeral home to bury the baby's father.

How did my life get so screwed up? Everything was going great. Perfect, actually. Obviously, we still had our ups and downs. Working minimum wage as a waitress while trying to get my husband, Adam, through college wasn't easy. But things were finally looking up!

We were accomplishing all our goals. Adam had recently graduated from college as an engineer and had received the perfect job offer. We were supposed to sign on the dotted line for the perfect little house, in the perfect little neighborhood, next week.

Everything *had* been perfect.

Fascinating how perfect can turn into devastating so quickly.

I'm standing in the bathroom of our tiny one-bedroom

apartment, trying to finish getting ready so I can get this day over with.

I refuse to look at the lime green toothbrush sitting on the chipped Formica counter next to the sink. I know that if I even glance in its direction, I'll collapse onto the cool tile beneath me, curl into a ball, and sob for hours. And while breaking down has been a common occurrence for the past few days, it's unacceptable this morning. I have somewhere I need to be, and I can't miss it for the world.

No matter how badly I want to.

As I wash my face with the cool water, I can't help but wonder, *What the hell am I going to do?*

I think I'm in denial. That's the first stage of grief, after all. Don't worry, I Googled it. Right after I Googled the accuracy of pregnancy tests. Apparently, they're pretty freaking accurate.

Dammit.

I look at the clock on my phone and notice I'm going to be late if I can't get my shit together and apply some more waterproof mascara. Waterproof means it shouldn't run right?

Maybe it's the hormones, but I haven't been able to stop crying since I received the call that my husband was killed by a stupid teen who couldn't stop texting for the ten minutes it took to drive home.

Now that I think about it though, a dead spouse seems like a pretty good reason to be losing it, emotionally.

I can't help but notice the bags under my eyes as I gaze into the bathroom mirror. The lack of sleep, and the constant crying, have definitely taken a toll. I try to take a deep breath while counting to ten, praying I can make it through the funeral without collapsing in front of everyone.

I start to leave the bathroom when I notice one of

Adam's socks laying in the middle of the floor, my eyes zeroing in on the worn black material. My balance is shaky and my breathing is shallow as I bend over slowly to pick it up. I hesitate before finally grasping the sock with sweaty palms and placing it in the laundry basket. Somehow, my mind knows that it's the last mess I'll ever clean up for him, and it guts me.

Knowing I need to be strong to make it through the day, I force myself to turn off my emotions, flipping a switch from agonizing heartbreak to blissfully numb. I'll deal with this pain tomorrow. I just need to get through today.

I lick my chapped lips then release a shaky breath before making my way to my car so I can head to my husband's funeral.

Walking into the funeral home, I can't help but notice the over-the-top flower decorations, and a cheesy picture of Adam in a gaudy frame on an easel by the closed casket.

I always hated that picture. It was so formal and so *not* Adam. His usually messy sandy-blonde hair is parted on the side, and his tie looks like it's choking him. His mother had insisted he have a professional picture taken for his résumé.

I avoid eye contact with my mother-in-law, Susan, who is standing next to the casket greeting friends and family of her deceased son. She's dressed in an elegant floor-length black gown and looks perfectly polished, even though I know she's heartbroken over her son's death. Adam was an only child, and Susan was constantly smothering him with her protectiveness and adoration. In her eyes, Adam could do no wrong...with the exception of marrying me.

To say I'm *not* one of her favorite people would be the understatement of the century. I was never good enough for her precious only child.

At least I wasn't the one who had to play referee between the two of us. I think Adam had it worse. The poor guy would spend every Sunday dinner juggling his disapproving mother and his cheeky wife. Is it my fault I refused to roll over and take her shit lying down?

I doubted I would ever see her again after today. Well, that had been my assumption anyway, until I'd seen those two pink lines this morning.

Is it wrong not to tell her?

I hadn't had a lot of say in the funeral planning. Not that I really minded, but Susan made it clear that I would've ruined it (her words, not mine). She was always so sure that I destroyed everything I touched. Like it was my fault both my parents had died, then my Grandmother when I was in high school, and now Adam. Now that I think about it, she might have a point.

It was a lovely service, if not a little cold. But what more could I expect from Mommy Dearest? The sweet stench of flowers and cleaning chemicals makes me gag. They weren't kidding when they mentioned super-human smelling powers when pregnant.

I need some fresh air. Now.

As I open the large oak doors of the funeral home and walk down the steps to help calm my rolling stomach, a familiar hand touches my shoulder gently. I quickly turn around and see Luke Jensen, Adam's best friend. My best friend, too, once upon a time.

He looks good. Really good. At just over six-feet tall with a muscular build, semi-short brown hair, and the greenest eyes you've ever seen, he's always been a favorite among the female population, and I can't blame them.

While I haven't seen him since our graduation five years ago, I can't help but feel the pull of our friendship like it was yesterday. Even if I am a little hesitant to rekindle it after his disappearing act all those years ago.

"Liv," he says, in his deep, familiar voice.

"Luke," I reply with a small smile.

"How are things?"

I look at him like he must be crazy.

"Really?" I reply, feeling the urge to cry and laugh simultaneously at his ludicrous question.

He runs his fingers through his dark hair and sighs.

"I guess that's not the smartest question, is it?" His lips tilt upwards on one side. "I'm really sorry about Adam, Liv," he says, sobering.

"I know." My eyes feel glassy. "It doesn't feel real."

I'm drained, both emotionally and physically. I walk over to a nearby wooden bench along the front walkway a short distance away from the funeral home. I motion for Luke to follow me, hoping to give us a little more privacy.

"What are you going to do?" he asks.

I assume he's talking about the house signing next week, and I let out an exasperated sigh, swallowing the lump in my throat.

I *wish* the new house was the only thing I had to worry about.

"I'm pregnant," I blurt out, shocked by my bluntness. I was never very good at keeping secrets from him.

Luke's eyes shoot to mine, but I can't hold his stare for long. I look to the cobblestone beneath my heels and pick at some non-existent lint on my conservative black knee-length dress.

I hear him curse under his breath before asking hesitantly, "Did he know?"

I bite my lip and slowly shake my head, avoiding eye contact.

"Nope. I found out this morning. He's not even here to crack a joke about how he slipped one past the goalie," I smirk at Luke, feeling a tear slide down my cheek.

He chuckles as he wipes the moisture away.

"Sounds about right." He smiles tenderly, and I know he's remembering his friend. Adam and his inappropriate jokes. I shake my head, fondly. I love that about him.

Loved. He's not here anymore. I sober immediately.

It's as if Luke remembers Adam's gone the same moment I do. His smile slowly disappears, and he asks again, quietly, "What are you going to do?"

I pause, trying to shake the overwhelming feeling of abandonment gnawing at my stomach.

What *am* I going to do?

"I don't know," I say honestly and shrug one shoulder. "What *can* I do Luke? How am I going to raise a baby? There's no way I'm signing on that house. Our apartment lease is up, and it's not like I can afford that now, anyway. I'm a widow. A *pregnant* widow," I laugh sarcastically, "with no place to live, no family support, no money, and a shit job that will barely cover my expenses, let alone a freaking baby!" I'm nearly screaming now and start to feel light-headed.

Luke pulls me into a hug, rubbing my back as I sob into his chest, pathetically.

I can't do this.

I can't.

"What about Adam's inheritance?" Luke questions.

I pull away from him slowly and give him a look that asks if he's joking.

"You know my beloved mother-in-law pulled that from him as soon as he proposed right? There was no way she was *ever* letting me touch her husband's precious money." I roll my eyes.

Ironically enough, Susan is also a widow, though not until after twenty years of marriage to a man she hated. I'm still not entirely sure she didn't poison him. Is it possible to die from being miserable?

Either way, while they weren't rich by any means, they were definitely comfortable. Unfortunately, Gregory didn't have a written will, *silly, naïve man*, so everything went to a woman he hated.

Susan had set aside money for her pride and joy, but as soon as he started spending time with the neighborhood charity case, aka me, she threatened to pull his inheritance. She kept saying his father wouldn't approve of the relationship, and therefore, she wouldn't financially support it.

It never mattered. We didn't need her money or her blessing. Susan quickly realized that if she wanted to keep her son, she had to be civil toward me. Although, *civil* might be an optimistic word for the relationship we have.

Had.

Our relationship died when Adam did.

I swallow the lump in my throat, feeling utterly defeated.

"So you really are up shit creek," Luke says, trying to lighten the situation.

"Yup," I reply, popping the 'p' at the end. "Without a paddle."

We both sit in silence, attempting to digest the newest development in my life that happens to be growing inside me. After a few minutes, Luke gives me a friendly side hug, squeezing me tightly before we head our separate ways. Because really? What else is there to say?

Luke

The funeral was hell. Seriously, I don't know how people do it. Go and say your goodbyes to a closed casket? Forced to accept someone is gone forever? No, thank you. I'd like to remember them living, not dead.

I think I'd prefer to skip the whole thing, actually. When I die, they can toss my ashes in the garbage. Let them think I moved to a nice, big farm where I have lots of room to run, like parents tell their kids when their family dog dies. Yup, I went off to greener pastures with the dogs.

I'm not usually such a pessimist. But Adam and I didn't exactly leave things in the best light. I had promised never to see him again, but he had to throw one final 'screw you' my way by dying too young and leaving his wife to fend for herself.

His *pregnant* wife.

Shit.

I loved him like a brother, but his betrayal still tastes bitter in my mouth, even after all these years.

I do miss him, though. Every. Single. Day. We'd been friends since kindergarten. He had thrown mud at me during recess, so I'd tackled him to the ground and ruined his new Spiderman t-shirt. We had been best friends ever since. Almost all of my childhood memories involved Adam in some way. It's hard to accept that he's really gone.

Then we met Liv.

I will never forget walking into my first period class junior year, right after Christmas break, and seeing the most beautiful girl sitting at a desk in the far corner. She was busy doodling in her notebook and refusing to look around the room, preferring to stay hidden behind her long, golden hair. I remember being so awestruck that Adam bumped me in the shoulder as he went to find a seat.

I'm sure you can figure out which seat he ended up choosing.

After that first day in school, the three of us were inseparable. Liv and Adam didn't start officially dating until he asked her to prom that same year. I had wanted to, but was too chicken shit to go through with it.

It was the second biggest mistake of my life.

My little secret that made me flee all those years ago after graduation was the first, and it's more than I can carry most days. I thought I had it under control. Until I saw her again.

She hasn't changed much in the last five years. Shorter hair with a few more highlights, and a fuller face, maybe. But other than that? She's still the same beautiful girl from high school. Even her dry sense of humor made an appearance once or twice today, which is a miracle considering the circumstances.

Those stormy gray eyes weren't as bright as usual, but they still sparkled like they held a secret. With the bomb she dropped on me, I guess they *were* holding a secret.

A big freaking secret.

I have no clue what she's going to do, but I know I need to stay out of it. It's none of my business. At. All. I fly home tomorrow night. I just need to make it that long before I can go back to my life...to Trisha.

It was hard enough to leave Liv the first time. It felt like I had lost a limb in the most gruesome way possible. My chest aches when I think of having left for college five years ago. I'm still not sure how I achieved it.

I'm sleeping at my parents' house while I'm in town. They haven't moved in twenty years. It's a nice little home, with a nice little yard, in a nice little neighborhood.

It's very *nice*.

I make my way down the hallway on the second floor, the walls lined with family pictures, and into my childhood room. I can't help the sense of déjà vu floating through my frazzled mind as I take in my Ninja Turtles sheets on a tiny twin-sized bed.

You'd think I would've changed the sheets to something more mature, but Liv got them for me as a joke for my seventeenth birthday. She said it would help me with the ladies. Not like I ever needed much help in that department, except with the one girl I couldn't have.

I shake my head in frustration, stripping down to my boxers before angrily turning off the lights and crawling into my Ninja Turtles sheets. In twenty-four hours I'll be home, and this will all be behind me.

CHAPTER TWO

LIV

The next morning, I lay in bed in my boxed-up apartment with tears rolling down my cheeks, missing Adam like crazy.

I have six more days until our lease is up. Six days.

Our tiny, one-bedroom apartment couldn't seem any bigger as I lay on our queen-sized bed by myself. *Maybe I should consider switching to a twin. That way I won't feel so small. So insignificant.*

I roll over to Adam's side of the bed as my tears soak his cold pillow. We always slept in and cuddled on Saturday mornings. I would tangle my legs between his to keep my toes warm. At some point while I slept, Adam would sneak out of the apartment and grab us bagels from the bagel shop down the street. I would wake up to kisses and the smell of his clean, spicy scent after his morning shower. It was my little slice of heaven.

Why did you have to leave?

There is still more packing to do, and I promised myself I wouldn't lie around moping today. Unfortunately, my queasy stomach has another idea. Looks like the couch and bathroom are going to be my best friends for the next three months.

Morning sickness is a bitch.

While splashing cold water on my face after puking for the third time this morning, I hear my doorbell ring. I make my way over to the front door and look through the peephole, seeing my savior standing there with saltines and 7-Up.

I swing the door open enthusiastically, not even caring that I haven't brushed my teeth, or that my shoulder-length blonde hair is sticking up in ten different directions.

"You are officially my hero, you know that, right?" I say excitedly, as I lean against the doorframe.

"Nice to see you too," Luke replies with a grin. "You look..." he pauses and grimaces as he sniffs the air.

"Yeah, I know," I interrupt. My super-human smelling powers are the first to detect the slight vomit stench still clinging to my well-worn pajamas.

"Go shower," he says with a sympathetic smile. "I'll start packing up your kitchen and then we can go to breakfast."

My stomach rolls at the mention of food, and an acidic taste immediately invades my mouth.

"Yeah...I won't be eating breakfast for at least a few more months, but those crackers look pretty tempting." I nod toward the package he's holding. "After my shower we can sit and catch up. Sound okay?"

"Sounds great. Where's your packing tape?" he asks, looking around the messy room littered with various moving boxes and packing supplies.

"On the counter under the microwave," I reply as I make my way to the bathroom. "I'll be out in a few."

"Take your time!" I hear him yell as I close the bathroom door.

The shower is an unexpected sanctuary, and I stay under the hot water until it starts to cool. After getting dressed in sweats and one of Adam's old t-shirts that still smells like him, I head back to the kitchen. Unfortunately, Luke is nowhere to be seen.

"Luke?" I call out, looking around the tiny apartment. The kitchen and family room are basically one large area, leaving him few places to hide.

"In here!" he yells.

I follow his voice and find Luke surrounded by boxes in my bedroom. All of Adam's drawers have been opened and appear to be empty. He's packing up Adam's clothing.

"What are you doing?" I whisper, hesitantly, taking in the scattered clothing.

Luke stops folding Adam's favorite basketball shorts and looks up at me sheepishly, shrugging one shoulder.

"I started in the kitchen, but figured you might need more help with his things." I can tell he's trying to gauge my reaction by the way his eyes scan my face.

Biting my lip, I slowly slide to the floor with my back against the wall near the bedroom door. I fold my legs up to my chest and drop my head in my hands. I can feel Luke's stare as I slowly wipe the tears with my sleeve.

I look up at Luke with glassy eyes, hoping his gaze will ground me. Taking a deep breath, I whisper, "I hadn't thought about that. I guess I figured Adam would take care of it when he got home." I laugh without humor and continue, "How pathetic is that?" I roll my eyes and place my head back in my hands, my shoulders shaking as I sob.

I hear Luke scoot closer. He immediately puts his arm around my shoulders and pulls me into him. I grab hold of the comfort he's offering and refuse to let go, sobbing into his navy-blue Henley shirt. Luke continues to hold me, mourning his best friend, while I mourn my lost husband.

It feels like hours until I can finally breathe normally again. It's a good thing I hadn't bothered with make up, or his shirt would be ruined. Regardless, you can still see my snot marks all over his chest. I look up at him with a watery smile and apologize for ruining his shirt.

He laughs. Hard. It's a full-on, slap-your-knees-can't-catch-your-breath kind of laughter. By the time he finally composes himself, he pulls me into him again and kisses my hair. I smile into his chest, craving the affection.

"Liv, my shirt is the least of your worries. I'm pretty sure this isn't the first one you've snotted all over, and it won't be the last," he teases, affectionately.

I sit up and giggle.

He's not wrong.

Luke was always my shoulder to cry on. Poor guy. Who would want that job?

Unfortunately, when I would have relationship issues with Adam in high school, he was always the one to calm me down and help me work things out. People might have considered him the "third wheel," but I liked to think of us as the Three Amigos. It was always us against the world. Adam was my boyfriend, while Luke was my best friend. We did everything together. That is, until he went to college in Denver. Not exactly close to us in good ol' Salt Lake City. After that, he fell off the face of the earth.

"Speaking of the least of your worries, have you figured out a game plan yet?" Luke asks, interrupting my walk down memory lane.

I scrunch up my nose and shake my head.

"Nope." I pop the 'p' sound to emphasize my point.

"Any ideas?" he probes.

"Nope," I repeat.

I look at him pointedly. "You were always the smart one...what do *you* think I should do?"

He stares into my eyes, and I can tell he's debating with himself internally. After what feels like hours, but is likely only seconds, he breaks our eye contact, rubs his hands through his hair then rests his arms on his bent knees.

"Stay with me," he states matter-of-factly.

I can feel my brows furrow as I give him a look like he's insane. He quickly grabs my cheeks, squeezing them together to make a fishy face and says, "Not like that. Geez, I just meant 'till you get back on your feet." He lets go of my face and stands, grabbing my hands and pulling me up with him.

"Adam wouldn't want you alone. He wouldn't want you to stress about how you're going to provide for his baby. He wouldn't want you homeless or working yourself to death *in order* to provide for his baby. He would want me to take care of you," Luke pauses, putting his lips between his teeth before finishing, "at least for a little while."

He's still holding my hands from helping me up, and I'm surprised at how close we're standing after his little speech. We're practically chest-to-chest.

He clears his throat and takes a step back, releasing my hands.

"Come stay with me." He shrugs. "There's nothing here for you."

I don't answer him immediately, taking a minute to consider his offer. He makes some pretty good arguments, but I'm not sure I can do that to him and invade his life so fully. What if he gets sick of me?

He left once. I'm not so sure I should rely on him again.

"Luke, I dunno." I bite my lower lip anxiously, actually considering his ludicrous proposal.

He's right. There's nothing here for me anymore. I haven't kept in contact with anyone since high school, not even Luke's family. When he left for Denver, we had promised to keep in touch, but life got in the way.

"Liv, what's there to think about? I have a three-bedroom condo begging to have a feminine touch. I work like crazy, and I would love some home-cooked meals on occasion." He nudges me playfully.

Luke was always a master at reading me, and he can see I'm starting to cave. "Good. It's settled," he declares, like I've agreed to this crazy plan. "Let's finish packing, then we'll get some food that won't make you puke, and you can call the movers."

He starts boxing up more of Adam's belongings like my major meltdown and our insane little agreement never happened. I grab one of Adam's ratty sweaters and slip it over my head, his familiar scent encompassing me and giving me the courage to accept Luke's proposal.

I nod my head slightly. *Well, I guess that's that.*

Luke

Shit.

Trisha is going to be pissed.

I honestly don't even know what to say to her. *What the hell was I thinking?* That one sentence has been going through my head on a constant loop as I try to digest the conversation I just had with Liv.

Why did I even go over to her apartment in the first place? I fell asleep last night with the determination of a workhorse, promising myself that I had done my duty by attending the funeral. That's all I'd needed to do. I was going to leave the past where it belonged...in the past.

I didn't need to go to her apartment with saltines and freaking soda. I didn't need to help her pack up Adam's things, and I definitely didn't need to be her freaking shoulder to cry on. I've never been able to watch that girl cry. It's like walking in front of a moving vehicle just to see if your body can stop the damn thing. Obviously it can't, and it hurts like hell.

But offering her a place to stay while she figures stuff out? That was *definitely* my dumbest idea ever. And yet, as I look back on my day of helping her, I can't help but think that maybe my not-so-brilliant idea was worth it to see her smile. Even if it was just a small one.

I take a deep breath in through my nose, dreading the conversation I need to have with my long-time girlfriend, Trisha. She's going to kill me. And honestly? I don't blame her.

Thankfully she doesn't know much about my relationship with Liv. Otherwise, I'm pretty sure Trisha will castrate me for offering her a place to stay.

Hell, she might castrate me anyway, once she finds out my new roommate is a gorgeous, newly single woman who I've known forever.

Not that it matters if she's single or not. Because it's not like she's *really* single. She just lost her husband who she's been in love with since she was sixteen. I don't know if you ever really get over that kind of thing. I sure as hell haven't.

It's not like it's my business anyway. All I offered was a room. That's it.

What the hell was I thinking?

CHAPTER THREE

LIV

After an outrageously expensive one-way ticket to Denver, we finally arrive at Luke's place.

As I walk into his condo, the first thing I notice is how this place could definitely use a woman's touch. It's gorgeous, but has he ever heard of a throw pillow? Or a picture frame?

Okay, maybe I'm being a little harsh. The place is beautiful, and it sure beats my old one-bedroom apartment. It's just a little too much of a house, and too little of a home, for my taste, but we can fix that in a jiffy. *Pier One, here I come!*

It looks like he's done really well for himself, though. I'm proud of him. The condo is amazing. The floors are covered in a dark hardwood, sleek granite covers the countertops, and modern leather couches separate the kitchen and family room. And don't forget the giant TV mounted to the wall above the fireplace.

He definitely has all the essentials covered.

"Wow." I whistle as my eyes scan the open floor plan. "This place is gorgeous, Luke!"

"Thanks," he replies sheepishly, placing a few of my

boxes on the kitchen island. Somehow, Luke had been able to coordinate our flight with the movers delivering my stuff.

"The guest bedroom is down the hall on the left, along with the bathroom. My office and room are both on the right," he says, leading me further into the condo.

As I pass the bathroom, my stomach rolls, and I'm reminded how well acquainted I'll soon become with his porcelain throne. I manage to take a few soothing breaths, preventing our inevitable acquaintance for a few more minutes.

Have I said it before? Morning sickness is a bitch. And did you know that it lasts all day? Yeah, neither did I.

He leads me into the guest bedroom (my bedroom?) and proceeds to tell me to make myself at home before he disappears to retrieve more boxes.

I look around the warm gray room, noticing a white four-poster bed with a simple navy comforter, and a matching white dresser and nightstand. The bed looks ridiculously comfortable as I stare at it from across the room. I can't resist the urge to fall onto my back and snuggle into the pillows, my eyes already growing heavy from lack of sleep and all the packing. I would kill for a good night's rest.

Luke walks into the room with more boxes, chuckling at my childish behavior.

"Still in love with your naps, Liv? I thought you'd have grown out of that."

I may or may not have a slight obsession with sleep. In high school, I refused to ever sneak out after curfew because I was looking forward to sleeping instead of breaking any rules. Luke and Adam never let me hear the end of it. There's just something about that feeling right before you're completely asleep, with your body melting into the mattress, the fluffy pillow cradling your head and neck, and the weight of the blankets wrapping you in a warm embrace.

I snuggle into the pillows more fully. I haven't slept well since I got the phone call about Adam. My mind hasn't been able to find a way to shut off. I've been stressed about trying to find a more permanent living arrangement, how I'm going to raise a baby on my own, what kind of job I need to find that's flexible, and the list goes on.

Somehow being in Luke's apartment causes my mind to finally give in and let me rest, and I would be stupid not to take advantage.

Instead of replying with a sarcastic remark, I just smirk at Luke and ask in a sugary sweet voice, "Could you close the door on your way out, Bellboy? I need some precious beauty sleep."

As I turn away from the door, snuggling into the sheets once more, I can practically hear the smile in his voice as he says, "Trust me Liv, you've had plenty of that."

The door quietly closes behind him, just as I begin to drift off to slumberland.

CHAPTER FOUR

LIV

I wake up to the sound of voices in the kitchen area. Peeking through the window, I notice the moon shining brightly in the dark velvet sky. I can't believe how long I slept; it must be ten o'clock or so.

At first I assume the voices are from the TV, but I quickly realize it's Luke and a woman. It sounds like they're having a heated conversation in the main living area.

I don't want to interrupt, but I really need to pee. I climb out of bed and make a beeline to the bathroom, but am stopped when I hear a feminine voice shout, "So *this* is the new roommate?" Her sharp tone is definitely accusatory and causes my hackles to rise.

I pause a few steps from the bathroom, trying to control my bladder and my raging hormones, before plastering a smile on my face and hoping it looks genuine. I turn toward the kitchen and see Luke in dark jeans, a light gray t-shirt, and messy hair sticking up in different directions. He must have been running his fingers through it before I came into the room. He does that when he's frustrated or nervous.

The question is, *why*?

My eyes bounce to the other person in the room, and I'm quickly met with a pair of scrutinizing chocolate-brown eyes belonging to a gorgeous woman. I try to be subtle as I look her up and down. Long black hair? Check. Legs that go on for miles? Check. Giant boobs? Double check. (Pun intended.)

Well, that does it. I'm officially intimidated.

Wait...why am I intimidated?

It's not like she's competition or anything, unless she was also hoping to stay in the guest bedroom? From the looks of it, I assume she'll be staying in the master suite with a certain someone who failed to mention a not-so-friendly girlfriend to his new roommate.

Scratch that. She *could* be friendly. Maybe she just didn't know her boyfriend invited his former best friend to move in with him because her dead husband knocked her up and then left her and.... I think I'm rambling.

"Hi," I say as politely as I can, waving my hand awkwardly. My eyes bounce between Luke and Miss Double D's.

"Hi," Luke replies with a hesitant smile. "This is Trisha. Trish, this is Liv." Luke makes the proper introductions, eyeing both of us warily. I can tell he's afraid a full-on chick fight is about to break out in his kitchen.

Trisha and I shake hands, and she seems much more polite all of the sudden. Maybe she's not quite as intimidated now that she's seen me with post-nap hair and smudged makeup.

"Liv, I was just telling Trish how we're old friends, and you were needing a place to stay," Luke says, holding my eyes with his own, letting me know he didn't go into all the gory details of my train wreck of a life.

"Yes," Trisha interjects, "he had mentioned getting a new

roommate who was an old friend needing a hand. What he failed to mention was that she was a girl." She emphasizes the word *girl*, almost like it's a four-letter word. I mean it is *technically* a four-letter word, but you get my point. I guess I would be pretty pissed too, if my boyfriend left that part out.

What she doesn't understand is mine and Luke's relationship. Or that I'm pregnant. Or that my husband just died. Trust me...I'm pretty sure I couldn't be any more *un*appealing to the opposite sex right now, even if I tried. And I'm *not* trying. At all. I may or may not have even showered for the past three days. Though to be fair, I *did* put on deodorant.

"It's nice to meet you," I announce, pasting the same uncomfortable smile on my face as before. I'm unsure if I should try to expound on my situation or not.

Trisha continues to stare in my direction, making me feel even more awkward than before. Does she expect more of an explanation as to why I'm bunking with her boyfriend?

The room is so silent I swear you could hear a pin drop. Luke clears his throat, but it does nothing to break the tension.

I've never been very good with awkward silence. I have a habit of saying the first thing that comes to mind in hopes of breaking it. I bite my lower lip, attempting to contain any possible word vomit. Unfortunately, it doesn't work.

"I'm pregnant," I blurt out, hoping to dispel any reservations Trisha has with Luke and I being roommates.

I see all the blood drain from Trisha's face, and it takes me a second to figure out why.

So much for helping Luke out with his girlfriend.

I was trying to explain how unappealing I currently am, but she may have taken that the wrong way.

"Oh no, no, no, no. It's not Luke's." I start to laugh, although there's little humor in it.

"It's..." I pause, Adam's name catching in my throat. My eyes become glassy as I glance at Luke. I'm not sure why I'm on the verge of an epic meltdown, but it feels like my heart is about to split in two. Obviously I know this baby is Adam's, and I'm still learning to accept that he's gone, but saying it out loud to an absolute stranger feels like pouring salt into a festering wound. It hurts like hell.

The silence grows, and I can tell Luke wants to save me from my embarrassment but doesn't know how. I'm light-headed, the blood is rushing in my ears, and my stomach is rolling. I'm about to lose it in front of someone I just met.

I shake my head, then turn to Trisha. "It was so nice to meet you, but I think I'm going to be sick." I rush to the bathroom and barely make it to the toilet before vomiting up what little I had eaten earlier today. I rest my head on the cool porcelain, letting the tears silently stream down my cheeks.

A few minutes later I hear the front door close quietly, then footsteps echo down the hallway. I'm too embarrassed to see if Luke is staring at me, even though I can feel his gaze. I decide to peek between my hands as I sit slumped against the wall, my elbows resting on my knees. Sure enough, Luke is leaning against the doorway staring at me, his thick arms crossed over his chest.

I pull my knees to my chest, attempting to make myself small. Or smaller, anyway. I've never been exactly big. At 5'2 and 120 pounds when soaking wet, there's not much to me. But today I feel like the size of an ant that just got squished under someone's big ugly shoe.

I'm crushed. Why do I feel like I just got slapped in the face with my dismal reality?

I'm mad, too. Furious, actually. How dare Adam leave me to raise a child by myself? How could he do that to me? The red-hot anger is boiling inside of me, threatening to take over until I make someone hurt as much as I am.

Apparently, I'm at the anger stage of this crazy grief roller-coaster.

Stupid Google.

I can handle being a widow at 23. It won't be easy. Damn near impossible, if I'm being honest. But I *can* do it. With time, I can get my life back together and move forward. Pick up the broken pieces and find some semblance of normalcy.

One day.

Having a child alone, though? That feels impossible. I wish Adam were here, just so I could yell at him. Scream until my voice is hoarse. Let him feel an ounce of the pain that I'm feeling. Why would he leave me? Why would he ask me to do this by myself? Why would he make an innocent little baby grow up without a father? How dare he!

Right now, all I'm feeling is hatred toward my dead husband, which is quickly followed by throbbing guilt deep in my soul.

I know he didn't want to leave.

But he still did.

I think I might puke again.

I heave into the toilet as the sobs wrack my aching chest, wondering if this pain will ever lessen.

I hear the doorjamb creak as Luke pushes off of it, making his way over to me. He holds my blonde hair back until I finish dry heaving.

Afterwards, he leans against the wall then slides his back down until he's sitting next to me.

He stays silent, leaving me alone in my thoughts for a few more minutes.

As the tears continue to slide down my face, Luke's deep voice finally breaks the silence.

"Do you remember that time, right before graduation, when I found you in the girls' bathroom?"

"Yeah?"

"Do you remember why you were crying?"

"Yeah," I repeat, breaking eye contact with Luke and staring at the far wall. "My Grandma had just died, and I was afraid I would be all alone. You were going away to college, Adam's mom was pressuring him to break up with me, again, and I didn't know what to do. I was so scared everyone would leave me. Everything was changing, and I didn't want to be alone." I peek up at him. "I needed you guys."

"And what did I tell you?" he asks quietly.

"You told me I would never be alone. You said Adam wasn't a dumbass, and only a dumbass would break up with me." I let out a light laugh, the tears drying on my cheeks. "You said that even though you were leaving for a little while, you would be thinking of me constantly, and that you would come back." I pause, turning my face toward Luke once more.

"I did say that." He pauses. "And did I come back?" he questions, his gaze piercing mine.

"Not by choice," I reply bluntly, my earlier laughter gone.

He didn't come back. He didn't visit. He didn't call. I never heard from him after he left. The only reason I ever saw him again was because his best friend died, and he was left to pick up the pieces. *Me.*

I stare at Luke, daring him to contradict me. He knows as well as I do that I never would've seen him again if it weren't for Adam's accident. I wasn't worth the effort, or at least that's how I felt. A lot of friends disappear after high school. I'm not naïve, and I couldn't care less about the majority of them, but I thought our relationship was stronger than that. He was my best friend. The one I could talk to about anything. The one I relied on for everything. But he left, and he never looked back.

"I couldn't come back. Not at the time." He hesitates, breaking eye contact and running his hands over his dark hair in frustration. "But that had nothing to do with you."

I wait for him to continue, not letting him off the hook. "Adam and I had a disagreement, and I didn't know how to handle it. I couldn't let it go."

"What disagreement?" I ask, my curiosity getting the best of me. I didn't know they'd had a fight. I would remember if there was something. I know I would.

"It doesn't matter anymore, Liv. What matters is that I never wanted to leave you. I wanted to come back, I just didn't know how. But I'm here now. I won't let you go through this alone, okay? I promise."

I feel my anger dissipate and rest my head on his broad shoulder as I pray that he keeps his word this time.

Luke

I'm in deep shit.

In more ways than one.

First, the whole Trisha thing. I was right in the middle of talking to her about my new roommate when Liv just *had* to saunter out of her room in one of Adam's old hoodies and shorts so tiny you didn't even know they were there due to them being swallowed whole by said hoodie.

And then, Liv just *had* to mention the pregnancy.

Obviously, Trisha jumped to the wrong conclusion. Her

assumption got Liv so worked up, I couldn't even focus on Trisha in order to set things straight. I practically shoved her out the door so I could check on the pregnant woman puking her guts out in my guest bathroom.

After seeing her sobbing, simultaneously breaking my heart and stirring up feelings that should definitely stay buried, I just *had* to promise her that I wasn't going anywhere.

I'm not sure I can keep that promise. Not while keeping my own heart intact.

And mentioning my disagreement with Adam?

What the hell was I thinking?

CHAPTER FIVE

LIV

Luke and I fall into a routine after the "Trisha Incident," as I like to call it. I never really see her, although Luke does have late nights often and sometimes doesn't come home until morning. I'm not naïve enough to wonder where he goes, or what he's doing.

I haven't really started looking for a job yet because morning sickness has kicked my ass. I've been living on the couch, nibbling saltine crackers and drinking ginger ale for the past six weeks. Thankfully, it's finally starting to get better, and I should be able to start looking for a job in the next couple of weeks.

Luke and I are sitting on the couch watching *Seinfeld* reruns before bed. My feet are in his lap while he's busy texting Trisha. Or I assume that's what he's doing. He keeps shifting in his seat and sneaking glances at me. He's not very subtle.

Are they talking about me?

"Your appointment is tomorrow, right?" he asks casually, while looking at his phone.

I can feel my forehead crease as I hesitantly reply, "Yes?"

Even though I answer, it's stated like a question. I have no idea where he's going with this.

"Mind if I join you?"

"Why?"

"I don't know. I was just wondering if you'd like some company." He's still looking at his phone like he's afraid of my answer.

"The baby's not yours so why do you care?" I don't mean it to come out so sharp, I'm just genuinely curious as to why he insists on being part of this pregnancy. And I may or may not be a little hormonal.

He finally looks up at me with his piercing green eyes. I can feel him looking deep inside me as if he's seeing past my armor and knows how hard it is to go through this pregnancy alone. He looks so serious, and I can see he's trying to find the right words to answer my overly blunt question.

After a few minutes, he finally replies.

"It doesn't matter if it's mine, Liv, the baby's yours. He, or she, is a part of you, and because of that one simple fact, I will care for both of you for as long as you need me."

His declaration stuns me into silence, and before I can really contemplate his answer, he changes the subject to a safer topic. He uses this tactic a lot. Whenever things start to get too deep or serious, he always finds a way to bring us back to our comfort zones and "safe" topics.

"So, what is the pregnant woman craving today?" he asks with a knowing smile, putting his phone down and massaging my feet.

I won't deny that I'm definitely pickier about what I want to eat now that I have a bun in the oven. He's had to learn the hard way that I change my mind constantly about what I'm in the mood for.

I've even managed to branch out with my eating habits a

bit lately. They're pretty random, though. Hamburger with extra pickles? Salt and vinegar chips with ranch? Hot chocolate with sprinkles? Yup.

Poor Luke. He's had a hell of a time dealing with these cravings, but it's definitely better than listening to me puke multiple times a day, so he's not complaining.

"A grilled cheese and..." I pause, considering my options, "some scalding hot chocolate pudding."

He throws his head back, laughing and shaking his head at my ludicrous request.

"Scalding hot, huh? Coming right up."

Luke gently places my feet on the couch as he stands and heads toward the kitchen, his charcoal sweats riding low on his hips.

"So...how's Trisha?" I ask, as I see his phone light up with her name.

He looks over at me, confused. "Fine, I guess. Why?"

"I dunno," I say, trying to sound inconspicuous. "I know I embarrassed you and all, but you haven't brought her around since *the incident*." I punctuate the last two words and make finger air quotes.

He smiles shyly and rubs his hand over his hair, avoiding eye contact.

"Well, I figured you'd want privacy." He shrugs.

Now I'm the one confused.

"Privacy? What are you talking about? This is your apartment. Did she come over here before I moved in?"

"Well, yeah."

"Then she should still be able to come over, Luke. Seriously. I know what boys and girls do at night. You shouldn't have to hide that from me. I get it. Hell, I'm pregnant remember? You shouldn't have to rearrange your entire life just because you decided to take in a charity case," I say, exasperated, pointing to my chest.

"You're not a charity case," he replies sternly. I can see his fisted hands on the granite counter.

He and I have had this argument multiple times. He refuses to let me help with the rent and even gets grouchy when I insist on cleaning or doing his laundry. I figure it's the least I can do. He's taken me in, pays for everything, and he even offered to go to my doctor's appointment with me.

He shouldn't have to give up his, *ahem*... extra-curricular activities, too. I mean, I know he's not giving those up, but it must be exhausting never being home and feeling like you have to tiptoe around your roommate all the time.

I jump onto my knees and lean over the back of the couch, resting my elbows on the edge. "Luke. Invite her over. I'm sure when you insist on being at her place all the time, it doesn't exactly give her warm fuzzies about you having a girl roommate. Maybe if she sees us together a little more, and makes *her* presence more known, she won't be so nervous or whatever," I ramble, trying to be diplomatic.

I don't know that she's nervous, but I have heard a few heated conversations when he's been on the phone. I can definitely put two and two together.

Luke clears his throat, nods, and then starts pulling out the ingredients for my grilled cheese.

I know I'm right. I just don't want him to regret asking me to stay with him. I have nowhere else to go, and I want to be as accommodating as possible. I owe him a lot, and if helping his relationship with Trisha makes his life easier, then it's the least I can do.

CHAPTER SIX

LIV

As we walk into the doctor's office, I notice how many of the women are alone. Some with swelling bellies, others without. I feel silly now for bringing Luke along, even if he insisted on coming in the first place. I can do this alone. I need to get used to it anyway.

The place is surprisingly busy with only a few chairs available. We find a love seat in the corner and sit down. I may have underestimated the size of the cushion because our knees are definitely touching. Luke doesn't move his away as he grabs a *Parents* magazine from a nearby coffee table, so I shrug off our close proximity, too.

I'm nervous. I guess that makes sense because this is my first appointment, but I still don't like feeling this way. I barely notice my leg bouncing before Luke lays his palm on my knee, rubbing his thumb back and forth. I'm wearing skinny jeans, and even though he's not directly touching my skin, his touch is still soothing.

I stare at his hand for a moment before hearing the nurse say my name.

I look up at Luke's face as he squeezes my leg and says, "You're up!" He starts to stand, but hesitates and asks, "Are you sure you're okay with me joining you?" His tone is so sincere. I know he would respect my privacy if I asked him to, yet I also know he genuinely wants to support me and come with me to the exam room.

I nod as I wipe my sweaty palms on my jeans.

Why am I so nervous? People get pregnant all the time. Nothing will go wrong. Everything will be fine.

And if it isn't, well, that would be more convenient now wouldn't it?

I shake my head, ashamed of my ridiculously negative thoughts. I feel tears prick my eyes as I let the truth grip me. I would be heartbroken if I lost this baby, even if he, or she, is making my life a billion times more difficult.

I grab Luke's hand and let the nurse lead us to our room, anxious for the doctor to reassure me that everything is right on track.

The exam room looks like any other doctor's office I've visited, and I take a seat on the exam table covered with the crinkly white paper. The nurse then tells me to change out of my pants and to put a blanket on my bare lap before quickly shutting the door behind her.

Luke shifts uncomfortably on his feet before pointing his thumb over his shoulder and mumbling, "I'll be right outside." Before he can get to the door, my nerves get the best of me. I grab his arm, my nails digging in to his tan skin, and practically yell, "Don't leave me!"

He chuckles as he patiently states, "I'll be right outside, Liv. As soon as you're changed, I'll come right back in." He looks at me reassuringly and speaks to me like you would a skittish animal.

I guess him waiting outside makes sense, especially

when I don't want him to see me naked. I just don't know how to handle the idea of being alone. And not just in *this* moment, but in the big scheme of things. It finally hits me that I really am going to have a baby by myself, and the one person who is here for me, won't always be. It makes me want to cry.

Again.

Damn pregnancy hormones.

I have to concentrate on releasing my death grip on Luke's muscular forearm as I mumble, "I guess that makes sense." I try to laugh to lighten the mood, but I know it sounds forced.

Luke turns around and faces me fully. He gently grabs my face between his two large hands. His calloused fingers softly scratch against my smooth cheeks, but I kind of love how comforting it feels; it feels like *my Luke*.

"I'll be right outside. I promise." He doesn't release me until I acknowledge that I understand his comment. I nod my head slowly and close my eyes, taking a deep breath. I feel his lips brush my forehead as he whispers comfortingly, "You can do this. Open the door when you're finished." Then he's gone.

I undress slowly, slightly ashamed by my neediness. Luke has a life outside of me and my drama. How can I drag him into this? I can't help but feel guilty. It's not his baby. He shouldn't feel obligated to be here, and yet he asked if he could join. It may be selfish, but I wouldn't have it any other way, and that scares the crap out of me.

After opening the door once I'm modest, or as modest as I *can* be while totally naked except for a piece of white polyester fabric on my lower half, I sit on the crinkly paper once more.

Luke smiles at me and takes a seat in the exam room

chair. He rubs his chin as if he's thinking about something important and asks, "Remember junior year in chemistry when you accidentally lit Rebecca Wells' hair on fire?"

I burst out laughing, staring at the ceiling as I ask, "Where in the world did that come from?"

He grins back and replies, "I dunno. I was just thinking about how much hotter she looked with short hair."

I can't stop smiling as I shake my head back and forth. "Dude. She had a giant bald spot afterwards. No matter how much her hair cut cost, there's no coming back from that." I continue laughing as tears roll down my cheeks. Happy ones this time.

This. This is why I missed Luke.

I never really understood how three people as close we were could drift apart like we did after high school. Well, like Luke did. Obviously, Adam and I stayed together, and we tried to keep in touch, but our graduation was the last time I saw Luke until the funeral. He even missed our wedding.

Luke opens his mouth to reply with an undoubtedly sarcastic comment when the doctor opens the door.

He's an attractive older gentleman with salt and pepper hair that is cut short. He eyes my chart before looking up and smiling at me.

"I'm Dr. Fellows. It's nice to meet you," he introduces himself, shaking my hand. "Congratulations on your pregnancy. Let's take a look, shall we?" I see him slip on some gloves then he lays me down on the exam table.

I'm not one hundred percent sure where he's going with this until he guides my feet to the stirrups. I quickly look over at Luke, seeing his face, on which there is what I can only describe as a "deer in the headlights" look.

He goes to grab the door handle attempting to make a

quick escape before my death grip on his forearm comes back with a vengeance.

"Don't you dare leave me!" I practically yell, again.

He looks at me like I must be crazy as he says, "You want me to stay?"

I know I must be as insane as he thinks I am because all I can do is nod frantically, refusing to let go of his arm.

Luke takes a deep breath, rubbing his palm over his face. He loudly exhales before whispering, "I won't look. Promise."

He continues to make eye contact with me as the doctor slowly lifts the blanket and proceeds to check me.

After he's finished, he puts the blanket back in place, and I hear Luke let out a breath he had apparently been holding.

Dr. Fellows proceeds to squeeze some cold stuff onto my lower belly and pulls out what I assume is an ultrasound wand.

After a few seconds, I start to hear a quick whooshing sound. It's loud enough that I break my eye contact with Luke as I shift my gaze to Dr. Fellows. He's officially gained my full attention.

"Is that...?" I don't finish my sentence, letting the words hang in the air.

The tiny rhythmic sound fills my ears and I'm immediately filled with a sense of awe and wonder. It's a feeling I know I'll remember for the rest of my life, one I will never take for granted.

"Your baby's heartbeat. Congratulations you two!" Dr. Fellows states with a giant grin.

I smile back widely before registering what he's said.

I feel my eyebrows pinch, my smile fading. You two? Who? It's just me.

Wait.

My eyes bug out of my head as I bounce my gaze between Luke and Dr. Fellows.

Again?

No.

No. No. No. No.

How do people keep confusing Luke for the dad?

"He's not the father!" I practically yell at the poor man before he quickly apologizes.

"I'm so sorry! I had just assumed...." He lets his voice trail off before I notice his gaze stuck on Luke's and my hands. Somehow our fingers have become tangled and are resting on the exam chair next to my hip.

I quickly release his hand and wipe mine on the top of my shirt.

Luke clears his throat loudly, running the hand I had been holding through his hair, again. He does that a lot around me. Remember how I said it's one of his nervous ticks?

Luke quickly comes to my rescue before I can have another meltdown, smoothing over the simple misunderstanding.

"It's an honest mistake," he answers for me. "Although, I would be *lucky* to call this baby mine. Thank you so much for your time, Dr. Fellows. I really appreciate you taking care of Liv for me. I'm sure we'll get to know each other well over the upcoming months."

I'm still lying on the exam table, trying to comprehend what he just said as my eyes bounce between the doctor and Luke again.

Seriously, I'm starting to get dizzy.

Luke notices my reclined state and helps me sit up, being careful to keep my lower half covered. I swing my legs over the edge of the table. His hand remains on my upper back as he holds my stare, silently questioning if I'm alright. I nod my head slightly before he finally releases his hold on me, stepping back toward Dr. Fellows.

"Well, if you need anything, be sure to let me know. Otherwise, I will see you in four weeks. Make sure you take your prenatal vitamins daily," Dr. Fellows says, reaching for the door handle. I can practically see the wheels turning in his head, trying to figure out who the hell Luke is, if he's not the father.

Dr. Fellows shakes his head and exits the room, quietly closing the door behind him.

"I guess we should've expected people to make that assumption. I'm so sorry, Liv. I'm not trying to make things harder on you. I just wanted to support you and the baby. I wanted to be part of this—as a friend." He rushes the last part out.

I shrug, trying to act casual. He's right. We should've expected people to make that assumption. Who wouldn't? He's an extremely attractive guy, holding hands with a girl at a prenatal appointment. He's got dark hair and I've got light. It's not like they would've assumed we were siblings.

I blow air out of my lips while tucking my hair behind my ear and trying to get a better grasp on my crazy emotions.

"It's not a big deal, and I'm glad you're here." I pause, giving him a shy smile. "Seriously, I don't think I could've done this without you. I know I need to get used to doing things on my own, but I really appreciate you being here for me."

I go to stand up and give him a hug before I realize I'm still very naked on my lower half. I barely catch the corner of the blanket as my feet touch the ground. I yank it up to keep myself covered, causing a slit to reveal my upper thigh. I then bend at the waist to use my other hand to clamp the rest of the blanket together near my knee.

I look up at Luke, my cheeks flaming, only to see his eyes glued to my now-covered legs. His lips are parted, and I can see his chest rising and falling quickly. It seems as if time stops, and I'm afraid I'll die from embarrassment before Luke breaks his stare and smirks at me saying, "I was planning on taking you to dinner after your appointment, but I didn't know I'd get a show, too."

I burst out laughing, grateful for his sense of humor at my awkwardness. "Well I plan on getting dessert!"

Luke

I can't believe I offered to go with her to the appointment. Really, I blame the app I downloaded. It went into way too many details of everything that can go wrong during a pregnancy, and how each doctor's appointment is supposed to go. What if they detected something was wrong with the baby? I couldn't let her go through that alone. After reading the details, there's no way I could do that to her!

But to sit in a room with a nearly naked woman that I've been in love with since forever? That was a different kind of torture. Thankfully, as soon as the doctor came in I was conveniently distracted. That is, until he left again, and she showed way too much skin. I try to remind myself that I've seen her in a bikini multiple times, but it doesn't seem to stop the image of her silky thighs from being ingrained into my memory for the rest of my life.

And then to be confused as the baby's the father? I couldn't believe how quickly my heart rate picked up at the idea of sharing the responsibilities of parenthood with someone as amazing as Liv. The elation I felt so intensely was quickly replaced by shame.

I'm starting to feel guilty for being here instead of Adam.

I shouldn't be here.

But I promised Liv.

The shame is gnawing at my conscience. I may have wished I was Adam in high school, but that doesn't mean I want to be a poor replacement for the guy. This is his wife. His child. He should be here.

I shouldn't be.

CHAPTER SEVEN

LIV

I t's been two months since my first appointment. I got a job as a receptionist at a law firm because Luke knew a guy needing some help. It's pretty boring work, but they're great about my pregnancy and have been really understanding whenever I've needed to miss work for my appointments.

Luke has insisted on coming to every one of them, and I can see Dr. Fellows and him developing a great relationship. Apparently, he told Dr. Fellows about Adam while I was getting dressed after my first appointment, and since then, Dr. Fellows has been really sensitive to my situation.

While I'm grateful for Luke's support and protectiveness, I often have to remind him that I'm not a delicate flower. I'm getting better. It's taking time, but I'm moving forward. That's the only thing I can do in my situation, and Adam wouldn't have wanted me to mourn him forever. It's only been five months, so I am definitely still mourning. But Adam was the happiest person I know, and he hated when I was sad. He would want me to be happy. Luke is good at reminding me of that.

He knows when I need a shoulder to cry on and will hold me, taking a walk down memory lane right by my side. He also knows when I need to take my mind off things. The stresses of today. The unknowns of tomorrow. That's when we go on adventures, which might be a trip to the zoo, or a last-minute run to the grocery store for ice cream and a movie.

Luke can look into my eyes and see exactly what I need. Hell, he doesn't even need to see me. I can send him a text and he just *knows*. It's a gift he's always had. I've never understood how he does it, but he just likes to call himself *The Liv Whisperer*. I like to call him *The Jackass*, although he knows I'm kidding.

I don't know where I'd be without him, and it scares me how much more I'm relying on him.

--

It's Thursday morning, and I have just finished putting on my fitted shirt and navy pencil skirt. I pause in front of the mirror, noticing the fabric stretching along my stomach. I'm going to have to get some maternity clothes soon. I'm excited to finally start looking pregnant, instead of like I just ate one too many pizzas.

Opening up my mascara, I start applying it to my lashes, my mouth forming a tiny 'o'.

I see Luke out of the corner of my eye in the mirror as he leans his shoulder against the doorjamb. He's dressed in a white button-down shirt with the top two buttons undone, his charcoal gray slacks molding to his muscular thighs. I rarely see him in anything but jeans and a t-shirt, and nearly poke my eye out as I take in his appearance. He looks good. Sophisticated. An alpha-male through and through. No wonder he has ladies chasing him left and right.

He clears his throat to get my attention.

"So, do you have any plans for tonight?"

I roll my eyes. He knows my only plans include a pint of Ben and Jerry's, yoga pants, and the TV remote.

"Why yes, I do. Did I forget to tell you? I'm going to the Ball. My fairy godmother asked me to be ready by seven." I bat my lashes at him, while giving him a cheeky grin.

"Perfect," he says. "But tell her that the pumpkin carriage won't be necessary. I'm more than happy to drive," he smirks back at me.

I feel my brows furrow, my smile sliding off my face.

Am I missing something?

"I'm sorry, what was that?" I ask, confused.

Luke laughs. "Seriously, be ready at seven. I'm taking you out. There's no way that much ice cream can be good for the baby, anyway."

He pushes himself off the door and places his hand on my belly, rubbing it like a genie might pop out.

I swat his hand away. "There's no such thing as too much ice cream, you silly man. Where are we going, anyway?" I ask, putting my hand on my hip.

He slips a piece of hair behind my ear, grinning mischievously.

"It's a surprise. But wear something other than yoga pants, will ya?" He winks at me before walking down the hallway, leaving me to my own thoughts.

Did he just make fun of my yoga pants?

"Jackass!" I yell in reply, his laughter echoing down the hall.

--

Later that evening, I'm busy staring at my closet, having no clue what to wear. "No yoga pants" isn't much direction, but I finally decide on a mint-colored sundress that falls just above my knees and does a pretty good job at hiding my baby bump. I almost feel normal as I pair it with some sandals and a simple silver necklace. My hair is down and curly, falling just above my shoulders.

I shrug as I look myself up and down. It's not like I'm trying to impress Luke. And yet, I want to feel pretty tonight. It's been a while since I had a night on the town.

That must be it.

I grab my clutch and walk out into the family room. Luke is sitting on the couch, staring at his phone. I can't help but assume it's Trisha that holds his attention. Does she know Luke and I are going out? It's not like it's a date. Obviously. He has a girlfriend.

He looks up, and I feel a little vulnerable as I see him slowly take in my appearance, starting with my toes. When he finally meets my eyes, I bite my lower lip and shrug my shoulders, mumbling under my breath, "Sorry I'm not a leggy chick with long dark hair and giant boobs."

I turn my eyes toward the floor, praying he didn't hear my ridiculous remark.

I'm nervous.

Why am I nervous?

This is Luke. *My Luke.* He's seen me puke my guts up, on more than one occasion, and pee my pants from laughing too hard. He's been there to hold me when I cry and to crack a joke when I'm grouchy.

What is wrong with me? All of a sudden, I feel like crying.

I think I just realized that he's not *my* Luke anymore. He's Trisha's.

This is ridiculous. Come on, Liv...buck up. Stop being so emotional.

Luke steps forward and gently tilts my chin up so he can see my eyes.

"Liv. If I wanted a leggy chick with dark hair and giant boobs, I would've asked Trish to go with me."

Shit. He heard me.

I feel my cheeks heat and try to pull away, feeling absolutely mortified and a little hurt, by how quickly he tore through my already shaky self-confidence. He grabs both sides of my face, making sure I have his full attention.

"You look gorgeous tonight. You are the most beautiful woman I've ever seen. I don't want to be with anyone else in the world, except you. And only you." He smirks. "And I guess your heirloom tomato can tag along, too." I snort, knowing he's talking about the baby.

He downloaded an app that sends notifications every week telling you how much the baby has grown, as well as the size of fruit or vegetable they are.

Apparently, my little one is the size of an heirloom tomato.

What the hell is an heirloom tomato?

Luke pulls me into a hug before kissing the top of my head, his lips lingering for a minute.

Hesitantly, he pulls away. "Come on. We don't want to be late."

--

We pull up outside a concert hall, and I give Luke the side eye.

"Seriously, will you just tell me where you're taking me?" I yell, exasperated.

He grins widely. I can practically feel his excitement rolling off him in waves, reminding me of a kid on Christmas morning. He places his hand on my knee and squeezes playfully after turning off the car. I yelp, pushing his hand away. He knows how ticklish I am!

Bastard.

"We, my dear girl, are going to experience something we've only ever dreamed about." He winks in my direction.

I raise one eyebrow at his cryptic statement, deciding he's absolutely crazy.

He grabs my chin, turning my face toward the windshield. Luke leans in, and I can feel his breath on my ear as he whispers. "We're going to see..." he pauses for effect, "Jerry Seinfeld."

I hear myself squeal in excitement before he even finishes his sentence, and I bounce in my seat eagerly.

I think I may have peed myself a little.

"Yes! Are you freaking serious? You can't be serious. I've wanted this for forever! How did you get tickets? How did you know about this? How did you keep it a secret?" I shriek excitedly.

He just smirks back at me, shaking his head back and forth and chuckling at my enthusiasm.

"So I take it this is a good surprise?" he asks me with a knowing grin.

"Hell yes, it is!" I say, doing another little happy dance in my seat. I can't contain my excitement as we exit the car. I jump into his arms and squeeze him so tight I'm afraid I might break him. Which is ridiculous since they guy is like solid rock. Still, my enthusiasm is contagious as he swings me around in his arms, laughing with me.

He and I have been watching *Seinfeld* reruns since forever. Adam always made fun of the fact that we were obsessed with a show that was as old as we were. But I just couldn't help it. I mean, it's a show about nothing. What's not to love?

--

Jerry was hilarious. Seriously. My sides still hurt from

laughing so hard. I even cried at one point. Although that may have been the hormones.

Regardless, it was one of the best nights ever. After the show, Luke and I went to a little Italian restaurant where I loaded up on breadsticks and alfredo. After the waiter cleared our table, I ordered chocolate cake for dessert. Luke enjoyed watching me eat enough for two grown men, let alone an heirloom tomato.

I don't ever remember laughing so hard in my life, and it wasn't just Mr. Seinfeld. Luke knew just what to say to keep me in stitches all throughout dinner.

As I'm finishing up my cake, convinced my smile is etched into my face forever, Luke grabs my hand on the table.

"Are you doing okay, Liv?" he asks, his face sobering somewhat.

I pause, seriously considering his question. The low-lit ambiance of the restaurant adds to the intimacy of the question.

"Yeah." I take a deep breath, slightly nodding my head. "Or at least, I think I'm getting there." Luke sends a small smile across the table, encouraging me to continue.

"It's hard, you know? And I'm sure it won't stop being hard, but I'm okay." I shrug one shoulder. "I'm having a baby and, even though I'm terrified, I'm excited too. I've always wanted to be a mom, and now I have the opportunity. It was like Adam's last gift to me, or something. At first I thought it was a curse, but..." I shake my head slightly, "I can't wait to find out if it's a boy or girl."

Luke's smile begins to grow, until it's covering his whole face. He squeezes my hand tightly.

"You're going to be the best mom, Liv. Seriously. I've

never seen a more incredible woman, and I can't wait to see you in action."

I blush at his compliment, lost in his intense gaze.

"I'm here for you, Liv. Always." Luke squeezes my hand reassuringly.

I nod my head again. "I know."

Luke

Last night was incredible. It couldn't have been more perfect. The show was awesome, and the company was even better.

It almost felt like a date.

And that is the problem.

We're not dating. At. All. This girl has more baggage than most people can carry, but that's not the problem. The problem is how much I want to help her hold all of it. I can't let myself get tangled up in her again. I can't.

I don't think I'd survive a second time. Scratch that. I know I wouldn't. This girl broke my heart and doesn't even have a clue.

I need to go see my girlfriend and forget all about the girl of my dreams. I need to leave those feelings in the past. Where they belong.

She doesn't need me to make her life any more complicated than it already is.

We're just friends. That's all she's ever seen me as, and that's all she ever will.

I definitely need to call Trish.

CHAPTER EIGHT

LIV

I lied.

When I said I was cool with Trisha spending the night in the room across the hall, I definitely lied.

It's been two weeks since our night out, and I guess Trisha got sick of being banned from the apartment. Or maybe Luke finally took my awful advice and invited her over.

Regardless, I'm lying awake in bed, and I can't help but hear them going at it like rabbits.

Seriously, with squealing, and thumping, and squeaking. Ok, maybe not *exactly* like rabbits. It's more moaning than squealing, and the squeaking is from the bed, not them. But you get the idea.

I'm pretty sure my cheeks couldn't get any redder. And these damn pregnancy hormones are *not* helping the situation. It's not like I'm getting laid anytime soon, and I've been pretty okay about it until I can hear what I'm missing out on from across the hall.

I can't help but notice the time, giving Luke a mental high-five for his stamina. And then, after realizing I just mentally high-fived my best friend for his bedroom prowess, I throw the covers over my head, even *more* embarrassed.

How am I going to face them in the morning? Do I ignore the situation? Comment on their performance? Maybe make a few suggestions that might enhance their experience? Uh...never mind. It sounds like I won't need to make many of those.

Gah.

I throw the covers off of me. This is ridiculous. It's 3:00 am, and I need to sleep. Luke needs to sleep. I feel like his mother. "*Sorry honey! Curfew! Time to finish up and go to bed now.*" I laugh dryly, knowing his mother has no idea how sexy her son is.

Wait.

Did I just say Luke is sexy? Nope. Not at all. These hormones are seriously messing with my brain.

I put the pillow over my head and try not to think about my *not-sexy* best friend doing it down the hallway.

--

The next morning I stumble into the kitchen in my sleep shorts and tank top, my hair a disheveled mess, and grab a glass of orange juice. My baby belly is finally starting to show now that I'm about halfway through my pregnancy. While gulping down my OJ, I hear giggling coming from down the hall.

Seriously? Again?

I roll my eyes as Luke's bedroom door opens and Trisha walks out.

Oh. Apparently, there's no round three for today after all.

Bummer.

She sees me at the kitchen counter and smiles. It almost

looks genuine. "Morning, Liv. How was your night?" She's definitely not as hostile as when we first met. I have to give her points for trying. I know it can't be easy sharing your sexy boyfriend with his high school best friend.

See? There's that word again. I have got to stop describing him that way.

"Just lovely," I say, as I try to maintain eye contact and not look too uncomfortable.

Her olive skin tinges with pink. "Oh no! I am so sorry if we made you uncomfortable!"

Well, so much for trying to look laid back.

I open my mouth to reply as Luke walks into the room, his hair still damp from a shower. He must not have had time to shave. I can still see his scruff from yesterday. He has a white t-shirt on and dark jeans that hang low on his hips.

He looks good. Really good. Apparently, sex is great for his beauty regimen.

I'm caught with my mouth hanging open as Luke smirks at me.

"Morning, Liv." He gives me a little head nod before turning to Trisha. "Ready to go, Babe? I don't want you to be late."

I have no idea what she's late for, but I suddenly hope her car breaks down on the way.

"Yeah, let me just get my stuff. Bye Liv!"

I wave awkwardly in the open kitchen. She grabs her purse and heads toward the front door as Luke trails behind. I try to stay focused on my orange juice, but I see Luke's strong arms wrap around her waist from the corner of my eye. She giggles again as Luke buries his face in her hair and kisses her neck. Trisha tilts her head to the side, granting him more access. I find myself staring for what feels like an hour, but surely must've only been a minute.

I think I might be sick.

Turning all the way around, I face the hallway instead of the make-out session by the front door.

I can feel my cheeks heating and decide to go hide out in my room. I pause mid-step, hearing the front door close. I'm not sure if Luke decided to walk Trisha to her car or not until I hear his footsteps on the dark hardwood floors.

I don't know why I feel like I just got caught doing something I shouldn't have. It's not like I was spying on them or anything, but I suddenly have a strong desire to blend into the cabinetry. Unfortunately, my hot pink tank top makes for horrible camouflage.

"Whatcha doin'?" Luke asks with a sly grin.

I've been caught. Doing what? I'm not exactly sure, but my cherry-red face is back with a vengeance.

"Nothing. I was just going to go take a shower," I say, speaking into my OJ glass, refusing to look at him. As I move to walk past him, he gently grabs my arm, preventing my escape.

"What's going on, Liv? You were the one who wanted me to invite her over here." His voice is teasing, but his eyes aren't. I can tell his question isn't rhetorical. Why am I struggling with this? It's not a big deal. He's never been one to shy away from PDA.

While Adam and I were together, Luke always had a revolving door of girls joining us for movies, date nights, high school dances, and the list goes on. I'd caught him, on multiple occasions, in compromising positions. It had never really bothered me then. Why is it bothering me now?

It must be those damn pregnancy hormones. That's the only conclusion I can come up with.

I shrug the shoulder he's still gripping, but he doesn't

remove his warm grasp. I hold his stare before licking my lips and whispering, "It feels different than before."

His eyes zero in on my mouth, neither of us moving. I suddenly recognize how close we're standing. I can feel his warm breath on my face and can practically taste the mint from his toothpaste on his lips. His other hand gently slides over my hip, turning me to face him more fully, our eyes never breaking contact. His thumb slips under the hem of my shirt and slowly glides across the sliver of exposed skin.

I know I should feel embarrassed for my proclamation, and I do. I have no idea where that came from, but I can't make myself break the spell that's come over us. I feel as though a dam is about to burst, and I'm not sure I'll survive the wreckage.

There's a knock on the door, causing us both to jump. Apparently, I wasn't the only one enraptured.

He clears his throat, releasing my arm before opening the door. Goosebumps erupt on my body from the loss of his heat.

"Hey Baby. I forgot my cell." Trisha walks over to the mocha coffee table and grabs her phone, her heels clicking on the floor. She turns around and pulls Luke in for another steamy kiss before walking out the door.

I squeeze my eyes together tightly, then rush down the hall to the sanctuary of the bathroom.

A hot shower is exactly what I need.

Or maybe a cold one.

Luke

Why do I feel guilty right now? Especially when it's for all the wrong reasons. I wasn't trying to shove Trisha in Liv's face.

I wasn't.

I was trying to put Liv back in the "friend" box, which is where she needs to stay.

The problem was how Liv looked when I walked in the kitchen after Trisha exited my bedroom. And the look on Liv's face when she saw me kiss her goodbye. That wasn't a friendly, *ew, kissing is gross,* face. That was an, *I'm jealous that wasn't me,* face.

And her confession? I felt as though she'd punched me in the stomach with her fragile little fists. What did she mean by that? "*It feels different than before?*" I wish I could read her mind, though I'd probably just be even more confused.

And that thing that almost happened afterward? That wasn't when I felt guilty. That was when all felt right in my world. She felt so perfect in my hands, her bare skin warm beneath my fingers.

Until I remembered the simple fact that she isn't *mine.*

And she never will be.

CHAPTER NINE

LIV

"Would you like to know the gender?" the ultrasound technician asks kindly.

Luke and I are at my 20-week appointment. I'm officially halfway through my pregnancy, and the baby is measuring perfectly healthy. I've been debating through the entire pregnancy so far whether I want to find out if my little bun is a he or a she. I don't know why I've been so hesitant to find out. Maybe it's because it will make my situation more real.

I'm also not sure what gender I'm hoping for. If I have a baby boy, will I just see Adam every time I look at him? And if I do, is that a bad thing? Or will it prevent me from ever moving on? Who will teach him to throw a ball or tie a tie? I don't know how to tie a tie! How do I not know how to do that? I'm sure there's a video on YouTube, right?

But what if it's a girl? She'll never know her father. She'll never have someone to threaten her boyfriends with a shotgun, or teach her how to drive. I mean, *I* know how to drive, but isn't that a dad thing? What if she turns out like my mother-in-law?

Shit. I think I'm hyperventilating.

Luke squeezes my hand and brings me back to the present. I look around the sterile room and at the black-and-white picture of my unborn child on the screen. I listen to my baby's thumping heartbeat echo across the otherwise silent room as the ultrasound technician waits for my decision.

Once again, I look to Luke for answers. He always knows what I need.

He's *The Liv Whisperer*, remember?

I'm overwhelmed, and I'm sure Luke can feel my anxiety rolling off me in waves, as well as seeing it on my face.

Luke slightly nods his head at me, silently acknowledging my indecision, before turning to the technician. "Could you write it on a piece of paper, and she can decide later if she wants to read it or not?"

I let out a breath I hadn't realized I was holding.

See? The man is a genius.

"That's a brilliant idea," I say, smiling at him.

--

Luke guides me out of the doctor's office after insisting on two copies of every ultrasound picture. I asked him why, and he just shrugged it off like it was no big deal, changing the subject like he always does.

He guides me out the exit with his left hand on my lower back, and holds out his arm for me to grasp once we step into the chilly air. It's cold for October, and the leaves are changing. It's one of my most favorite times of the year. I can feel the cool breeze through my coat as I cling to Luke's bicep for warmth, resting my head on his shoulder.

It's nice having someone to lean on, both figuratively and literally.

The last few years were hard on Adam and me as he was

finishing up school. I often went to bed and woke up alone. He was always studying for a test, a quiz, or an exam, or working on a paper, midterms, finals... you get the idea. I knew it wouldn't always be that way, but it was draining. Sometimes, late at night, I would lie awake wondering if the loneliness would ever end.

We were so close to finishing and moving forward to a happier time. It feels like my dreams slipped through my fingers.

I cling to Luke harder, praying he doesn't slip away, too.

--

The next morning I'm sitting at the kitchen table eating Captain Crunch while wasting time on Facebook. Trisha exits Luke's room, saying goodbye as she grabs her purse.

I wave my spoon in her direction, unable to verbalize my goodbye with my mouth full of cereal.

I look back at my phone before Luke pulls out the chair beside me, the legs scraping against the floor. He grabs the Captain Crunch box and sticks his hand inside, grabbing a handful and shoving it in his mouth.

"I sure hope you washed your hands after last night's activities," I tell him sardonically.

He rolls his eyes before talking with his mouth full, "I don't know why you don't just buy the *Oops! All Berries* kind. Who likes the yellow squares, anyway?"

I grab the box back from him, pouring myself another bowl. "I like the yellow squares," I tell him. "And why don't you learn to buy your own damn cereal?" I ask with a cheeky grin, letting him know I'm teasing.

He grabs it back from me, pouring cereal straight from the box into his mouth. A few pieces land on his shirt. After chewing for a few seconds, he says, "I do buy my own cereal.

It's just not as good as yours." Luke smiles, his teeth covered in breakfast cereal. He picks up a piece from his shirt, throwing it in my direction.

I catch the cereal in my mouth, crunching it loudly. "Touché."

"So, what are your plans for tonight?" Luke asks after swallowing his Captain Crunch.

"Not much. Maybe *Hocus Pocus* if I'm feeling extra spooky." I wink at him.

It's Halloween, and I obviously don't have any plans.

"You want to come hang out with Trish and me?" Luke asks as he kicks his feet up on the chair opposite him.

I snort. "Yeah, I'm sure Trisha would *love* me being the third wheel."

He bounces his eyebrows up and down. "Well, she's always wanted to try a threesome."

I choke on my bite of cereal, unable to stop coughing.

I'm sorry...can you repeat that?

"Geez, Liv. I was kidding! If I knew you were that into it, I would've mentioned it sooner!" Luke teases, patting my back as I continue wheezing.

I take a swig of milk from the carton, then gasp for air. It's usually one of my pet peeves, but desperate times call for desperate measures.

Once I catch my breath, I hit Luke in the shoulder. "That's disgusting, Luke! And I'm pretty sure my belly would just get in the way, anyway." I start rubbing it playfully, while giving him a saucy grin.

Luke and I used to play a game kind of like "chicken" in high school. We would always try to embarrass the other one by flirting and making inappropriate jokes. The first one to blush or cave to the uncomfortableness was the loser.

Luke has always been the dirtier one, so I almost never won, but sometimes the stars would align, and I would get the best of him. I feel like today might be one of those times.

His eyes narrow, and he licks his lips. "I'm sure we could get creative."

I bite my lower lip, trying to contain my laughter as I take it a little further. "Let's try some right now. If you're not too busy." I give him a smoldering look, making sure my voice is breathy.

"Sweetheart, I got all morning," Luke says with a cocky grin.

I place my hand on his thigh, leaning in. I look up at him through my long upper lashes before licking my lips. "Good. Let's get started," I whisper, closing in on him.

His right hand grasps the side of my jaw, his fingers tangling in my hair. His left hand lands on the arm of the chair, leaning on it as his face inches closer.

My eyelids start to get heavy as I glance at his luscious lips.

We're so close I can practically taste the sweet cereal on his tongue. I notice I'm holding my breath.

I forget the game we're playing, silently begging Luke to lean a little closer. I bite my lower lip, unable to handle any more torture. His thumb gently pulls it from between my teeth, inching closer until our lips are nearly touching.

Is it hot in here? I feel like I just might catch fire from his molten gaze alone.

That is, until Luke smirks once more, dropping his hand from my face. "I win," he says, grabbing a yellow square from my bowl and popping it into his mouth. He acts as though he didn't just turn my entire world on its axis in a few short minutes.

I swallow loudly. A blush creeping up my face.

Dammit.

Luke

My morning conversation with Liv definitely brings back memories. The best kind of memories. I love being able to flirt with her, hiding my true feelings behind a sorry excuse of a game of chicken.

That girl has no idea.

I'm freaking proud of my self-discipline though. Resisting the urge to kiss Liv when I feel like that's exactly what I was made to do. I can still feel her silky skin in my hands. I can taste her breath on my tongue. She would taste so *sweet,* and she looked ripe for the picking.

I shake my head in utter shock. I almost freaking kissed Liv. *She was right there.* I pull my hair in frustration and let out a deep, shaky breath.

We've played that game so many times in the past, but it's never gotten that close before. The girl would blush at the mere mention of a threesome, let alone allowing me to touch her.

I shiver at the memory.

So close.

I'm glad she didn't agree to come with Trisha and me. I don't mean that harshly, it's just I think I'm needing some alone time with my girlfriend so we can reconnect.

Liv moving in has put a lot of strain on our relationship, and I need to focus on what's most important. I can't let Liv turn my life upside down any more than she already has. I'm happy to help her, but I still need to keep things in perspective.

I'm not in a relationship with Liv. I'm in a relationship with Trisha.

I keep repeating that mantra as I get ready for the evening.

You'd think that I wouldn't have to keep reminding myself.

CHAPTER TEN

LIV

I politely refused to go out with Luke and Trisha, especially after our threesome conversation. I mean, really? How awkward could I make my life? Maybe I should've gone and flirted with Trisha, just to see Luke's face. Then again, it probably would've backfired, just like this morning had.

Regardless, I'm asleep on the couch, surrounded by candy wrappers after binge-watching Netflix, when I hear the front door slam. I jolt awake, afraid it's an intruder.

I peek over the side of the couch to see Luke leaning against the wall by the front door. His head is tilted up at the ceiling, and he looks exasperated. Luke runs his fingers through his hair, pulling on the roots, before rubbing his face harshly.

He and Trisha dressed up as Edmond Dantes and Mercedes from *The Count of Monte Cristo*. I'm not sure how she convinced Luke to dress up as Edmond, especially since they don't end up together at the end of the book. I bet she just watched the movie. She definitely pulled off the look in an 1800's tight red gown with deep red lipstick, though.

I'm surprised Luke's lips aren't stained the same color.

Then again, it *is* pretty dark in here, so who knows?

He's still in his blood-red doublet, a crisp white button-up shirt underneath, with black pants. He looks like a sexy pirate. His hair is a tussled mess from running his fingers through it so many times.

I can't help but check him out as I take in his roguish appearance. He looks like he just stepped out of a historical romance novel. I subtly wipe my mouth, checking for drool.

Phew. No slobber.

I'm surprised he's home. I had assumed he would just stay over at Trisha's place. Or that they'd both end up here. *Again.*

"Hi," I whisper, still peeking over the couch.

Luke jumps, his eyes finding me from where he leans against the wall. He exhales loudly through his mouth, blowing out his frustration.

"Shit, Liv. I didn't see you."

I scoot up the rest of the way and lean my elbows on the couch, still wrapped in my dark purple comforter that I added to the family room as a nice woman's touch.

See? I haven't been a completely worthless roommate.

"Sorry," I apologize. "I didn't mean to scare you. What's up?" I ask him, taking in his frustrated expression.

"Nothing." He pushes off the wall, shrugging as he walks over to the kitchen and grabs a drink from the fridge.

"You sure? Why are you home? Where's Trish?" I don't mean to interrogate him, I'm just curious. He looks like he's had a rough night.

I look at the time on the microwave. It's 3:00 am.

Luke takes a long pull from his bottle of water before placing it on the counter and wiping his lips with the back of his hand.

I sit, staring at him. I can feel him battling with himself about something. Although, I can't figure out what it is for the life of me.

After what feels like forever, he grabs the bottle off the counter and walks over to me.

"Nothing," he repeats, sitting on the couch cushion beside me.

I twist so that I'm facing him, my legs curled up underneath me. Resting my head on my hand, my elbow sitting on the back of the couch, I wait for him to expound.

"Want to talk about it?" I whisper, quietly. I can feel his inner turmoil as if it's my own.

There's something so intimate about this moment. The room is dark except for the streetlight from the window casting shadows throughout the room. The quiet ticking of the clock hanging on the wall. The steady breathing of my best friend as he sits beside me. The heat radiating off his body as he leans his back against the couch, getting comfortable, yet looking utterly defeated.

He hangs his arm behind the sofa, grazing my upper arm, and shakes his head.

"Trish and I had a fight."

I raise my eyebrows, waiting for him to continue. Fighting hasn't exactly been an uncommon occurrence between them since I've moved in with Luke.

Luke moves his arm from behind me, leaving goosebumps in his wake. Leaning forward, he places his elbows on his knees, his head in his hands.

"I did something really stupid." He laughs, but there's no humor in it.

"That's not hard to imagine," I tease. "What'd you do?"

He takes a deep breath before mumbling into his hands, "I may have called her the wrong name during sex."

I can feel my eyes bug out of my head as my jaw hits the floor.

What?

He laughs again before finally looking at me.

"Yeah. I know. Not my best moment."

I'm speechless.

Seriously, I'm one hundred percent out of words right now.

And the only question that keeps running through my mind is, *What the hell did you call her?*

Nope. I'm not sure I want to hear the answer to that question.

I realize my mouth is still hanging open so I try to smooth my features. I pull my knees to my chest and lean my shoulder into the cushions. I'm still fully facing him, but I feel the need for a barrier between us, my blanket and legs seeming to do the job. I rest my chin on my knees, biting my lip.

The silence hangs heavily in the room as Luke waits for me to say something.

"That probably wasn't the best idea."

No shit, Sherlock.

He laughs again, rubbing his hands over his face.

"Yeah. I know."

"What were you thinking?" I ask him, shaking my head slightly.

"I wasn't thinking!" he yells, exasperated. "We were in the moment, going at it, and..." he hesitates, "it just came out."

"Well, what did you call her?" I ask, before biting my tongue.

Oops. I thought I wasn't going to ask that!

Luke's cheeks instantly turn bright red, his eyes darting

around the room. He takes another swig from his bottle before clearing his throat.

"It doesn't matter, Liv. What matters is that I'm screwed. Seriously, who does that? Obviously, Trisha's pissed. She kicked me out, with good reason, and wants to talk about it tomorrow once she calms down. I know she's going to break it off. I mean, who wouldn't? I was such an ass. How could I do that to her?" He shakes his head, disgusted with himself.

I unfold myself from my guarded position, tucking my feet beneath me again. I gently touch Luke's shoulder, getting his full attention.

"Are you sure you should be in a relationship with her when you're thinking of someone else when you're with Trish?" I whisper, quietly.

His bright green eyes focus on mine; he leans a little closer.

"Probably not," he breathes, his Adam's apple bobbing in his throat as he swallows. I can feel his breath on my cheeks, suddenly aware of how close our faces are.

Luke gently touches the side of my face, pulling me closer to him before leaning his forehead against mine. He closes his jade-colored eyes, squeezing them shut tightly as if in pain.

"I'm sorry," he sighs, sounding defeated.

I shake my head, pulling back from his close proximity.

"Sorry? What the hell do you have to be sorry for?" I can feel my brows furrow, confused at the turn of events.

I had *kind of* thought he was going to kiss me.

Which is ridiculous.

I shake my head slightly and wait for Luke to explain his apology.

"It's just..." he pauses, "you've got enough on your plate.

You don't need me throwing all my baggage at you, too." He grunts.

I shake my head, a small smile playing on my lips. "Seriously, Luke? If anyone should apologize for throwing baggage, it's me." I chuckle. "Who's the pregnant widow sleeping in your guest bedroom for the foreseeable future?" I point to my chest, smirking.

He rolls his eyes, laughing. "You're more than that, Liv. And we both know it."

I hold my breath, trying to understand any hidden meaning in his statement before he quickly clarifies, "You're my best friend, too." He shrugs.

Oh. Right.

I nod, pasting a smile on my face again.

"Yup. And as your friend, I'm telling you that you're welcome to throw your baggage at me, anytime. Anywhere." I smirk at him. "And speaking of baggage, I've decided I want to know the gender." I look at him through my eyelashes, anxiously waiting to see what he says. I don't know why I feel nervous telling him, but I'm starting to feel like he's invested in this pregnancy too, and his opinion matters to me.

His face transforms into a huge grin. "That's great, Liv! Seriously! Where's that damn piece of paper? Let's read it right now!" He shoves me softly, yet playfully, off the couch.

I laugh before grabbing my purse off the kitchen counter. My hands shake as I unzip the front pocket. I've been carrying around this stupid piece of paper since my appointment, too afraid to read it.

Taking a deep breath, I hold the note to my chest and glance at Luke. He nods encouragingly at me while patiently waiting for me to unfold the paper and read the results.

I smile at him nervously before squaring my shoulders and opening it. Licking my lips, I take in the four simple words written in swirling cursive.

It's a boy. Congratulations!

I feel like the world stops spinning as I try to digest the short sentence. The note is shaking in my hands as a tear slides down my cheek, blending the ink into the paper. I'm not sure if it's a happy tear or not.

I'm so overwhelmed. My feelings bounce between excitement and nervousness so quickly, I think I might throw up. How am I going to be a mom to a sweet little boy without a father? I've never felt more alone. This is harder than when I saw those two little pink lines all those months ago. It didn't feel real then, but it feels real now. It feels so real in fact, that I feel like the wind just got knocked out of me.

I squeeze my eyes shut, afraid I might pass out. Then Luke's arms surround me. He pulls me into an embrace that feels like coming home. He rests his chin on the top of my head as he gently sways me back and forth.

Luke continues to rock me as I silently cry into his chest, ruining his costume. I'm not sure how long we stay like that, but I finally feel my tears starting to dry.

He slowly runs his hand up and down my back before mumbling into my hair, "I'm embarrassed."

I shake my head back and forth, wiping a little snot on his doublet. "Why on earth are you embarrassed? I'm the one that's embarrassed," I murmur into his chest, too humiliated to look at him.

"I'm *embarrassed*," Luke emphasizes, "because I'm always bragging about how I'm *The Liv Whisperer*, and yet I have no clue what to do right now." He chuckles, nervously. "Are you having a hermaphrodite? Is that why you're crying? 'Cause I honestly don't know how having a healthy boy or a girl could possibly be a bad thing," he jests, trying to lighten the mood.

I giggle into his chest. Little does he know, *The Liv Whisperer* has succeeded again just by holding me close and momentarily releasing the iron fist in my gut by making me laugh.

I stay silent, pulling away from his chest just enough to hand him the paper before burrowing back in. I hear the paper crinkle slightly as he reads the results.

I'm wearing one of Adam's worn t-shirts that practically swallows me whole. The neckline must have slipped off my shoulder at some point. I hadn't noticed until I feel Luke bend forward, brushing his soft lips against my exposed skin. Goosebumps race across my flesh as his breath tickles my ear.

"He's going to be perfect," Luke whispers affectionately, his rough stubble scratching my cheek as he lifts his face to mine. "Just like his mom." He kisses my forehead softly, lingering a moment before lightly touching my cheek with his hand.

Luke takes in my face, puffy from crying, his lips tilting at the corners.

"I hope he has your eyes," he states, looking deep into my blue-gray irises. "I've always been a sucker for a good summer storm." His gaze is so intense I can feel it in my soul. I start to think he might kiss me. My mind races as I stare at his soft lips, unsure if I want him to lean in or not. Whether he should close that small gap.

Would I kiss him back?

Would I give him the cheek?

Should I give him the cheek?

His smile falters as he stares at my mouth before his lips

turn into a full-on grin. "Let's just hope he doesn't get Adam's goofy ears."

I snort, laughing at Luke's joke, the spell now broken.

"Come on, Beautiful. Let's get you some rest." He grabs my hand, leading me to my bedroom.

As we make it to my doorway, he releases my fingers and leans on the doorjamb. "You're going to do awesome, Liv. And you won't have to do this alone. I'm here for you. I always will be."

With that, he raps his knuckles on the door before making his way to his own bedroom, his door quietly closing behind him.

"I hope so," I whisper to myself.

Luke

I bang my head quietly against my closed bedroom door, trying to knock some sense into my pathetic brain.

I'm falling.

Again.

I can feel it. But no matter how hard I try to stop, it's happening. I feel like I'm dangling off a cliff, my hands scraping against the rough dirt, the ground caking beneath my fingernails, but I can't seem to find a strong enough grip to pull myself back up. To back away from the ledge and head toward safety, where my heart won't be obliterated.

Again.

Instead, I'm clinging uselessly, prolonging the inevitable.

I'm going to plummet to my death, and the only person I can blame is myself.

It's not her fault she's perfect. That she's beautiful, loving, kind, gracious, caring, thoughtful...I could go on.

I shake my head in frustration before sliding to the floor, defeated.

He's always going to have her heart. It will never be mine, no matter how much I want it to.

I just wish I didn't have such a hard time reminding myself of that.

CHAPTER ELEVEN

LIV

The next few weeks go by quickly. Neither of us mentions the *almost* kiss. Maybe that's because it was all in my imagination to begin with, which means there's nothing to mention in the first place.

I'm starting to feel Little Man wiggle, and it's the best thing ever. Apparently I've been feeling him for a while now, and I just didn't know it was *him*. Nevertheless, it's awesome, and it totally makes puking my guts out for three months worth it.

Luke and Trisha broke up, which I think is probably for the best considering Luke's little slip-up. And we've been having fun hanging out, just the two of us.

Not going to lie, it's been awesome.

We've gotten into a routine of taking turns cooking dinner and watching *Seinfeld* or *The Office* every night on the couch.

I also haven't cried since finding out my baby is a he, so I consider that a win, too. Maybe these pregnancy hormones are finally leveling out.

Hallelujah!

I think it definitely has something to do with my best friend being back. He was always *there* when I moved in, but since breaking up with Trisha, it's like he's stopped holding back or something. I'm not really sure how to explain it, and I can't quite put my finger on it, but I think I like it. Scratch that, I *know* I do.

We have deeper conversations, diving right in, instead of scratching the surface and tiptoeing around certain subjects. Like Adam. I'm learning how to talk about him without breaking down into tears, which is an accomplishment in itself. Luke knows Adam was a huge part of my life and doesn't get jealous when I talk about my relationship with him.

It's therapeutic talking with Luke. I kind of love it, actually. It's been great to see how much he's changed, while still holding on to some of the same old Luke from high school.

A few nights before Thanksgiving, we're binge watching a show on the couch when I feel my Little Man wiggle again. I'm lying on the couch with my legs in Luke's lap, a bowl full of popcorn on my chest. I quickly grab Luke's hand and shove it onto my stomach, spilling kernels everywhere.

"He's kicking!" I announce excitedly.

Luke's brows pinch in concentration, waiting for Little Man to move. For some reason, Little Man has been stubborn and refuses to kick when I actually want him to, so Luke hasn't felt him yet.

I watch Luke's face, my hand over his as he gently rubs my belly. I'm getting used to strangers touching my swollen stomach, but it's different when Luke does it. It's more intimate, I think. Like he's trying to connect with Little Man, as well as with me. He's not just feeling it out of curiosity or obligation. He's genuinely trying to form a relationship with the little person growing inside of me. It kind of makes my heart melt.

"Hey Little Man," Luke whispers, bending closer to my stomach. "I'm Luke. I know we've talked a few times before, but I think you got your stubborn gene from your daddy," he jokes. "Do you think you can give me a little hello?" He waits patiently. I can feel the heat of his hand through my thin cotton shirt. "Please, buddy?"

I wait anxiously, praying my Little Man will throw Luke a bone.

No movement.

He waits another minute and still doesn't feel anything.

After a little while longer, Luke starts to remove his hand from my belly. He looks at me, trying to hide his disappointment, and shrugs. "I guess he doesn't like me," he jokes, the right side of his mouth tilting up a little.

I give him a small smile before lifting my shirt and grabbing his calloused palm again. I place it on my bare stomach and nod encouragingly. His hand practically covers my whole core. "Keep trying, Luke. I never knew you were a quitter," I tease, a smirk gracing my lips.

Luke laughs before scooting closer to my tummy. "Hear that Little Man? Your mom thinks I'm giving up on you. Little does she know, I've only given up one thing in my entire life, and it's the biggest regret I've ever had." His voice starts getting quieter, like he's sharing a secret with my belly button. "And I'm not going to make that same mistake again." His brilliant green eyes peek up at me, before he focuses on my stomach again.

I feel myself practically begging my unborn child to move. A nudge. A kick. A flutter. *Anything.* "Come on, buddy," I whisper under my breath, my eyes zeroing in on Luke's calloused palm.

After a moment, right when I'm about to tell Luke to try again later, I feel it. A tiny flutter on my right side.

Luke's face lights up as he stares at my stomach in awe.

"Did you feel that?" he practically yells excitedly.

The baby kicks again, right on his index finger.

"He did it again!" he shouts triumphantly. He places his other hand on my belly so that both hands are fully covering my round stomach while the little guy goes to town twisting and turning as if dancing to music only he can hear.

The grin on Luke's face is the biggest I've ever seen. It's so contagious that my own cheeks start to hurt from smiling so hard.

It lasts for a few minutes as Luke laughs repeatedly from excitement. When Little Man starts to calm down, Luke leans forward and kisses my bare stomach softly. "Thank you, Little Man," he whispers, sincerely. "Thank you so much."

Luke

A little boy that isn't mine just stole my heart. Sounds cheesy, I know. I haven't met him yet, not formally anyway. But with each tiny movement I feel, with each time I listen to his little heartbeat thumping away, I fall a little bit more.

I'm not trying to replace Adam this time. I'm not stupid enough to think I could ever fill those shoes. But I can love him anyway.

I can be Uncle Luke, or something.

All I know is that this kid is stuck with me, whether he likes it or not.

And I can't wait.

CHAPTER TWELVE

LIV

L uke decides to stay home for Thanksgiving instead of heading to Utah to see his family. He'll be visiting them during Christmas and doesn't want to travel twice. Luke invited me to tag along in December, but I haven't decided if I'll join him or not. I know his family well and would love to see them, but it's a little too close to my mother-in-law, Susan.

I still haven't told her about the baby. I know I should, and I will. *I think.* I just haven't worked up the courage to confront her yet. Adam was an only child, which means this baby will be Susan's only grandchild, her only living family. Except me, but I don't count. I'm not sure how much input I want her to have in Little Man's life, or if I want her involved at all. But now I'm almost seven months pregnant, so time is definitely running out.

We spend a quiet day at the condo for Thanksgiving. We order Chinese instead of cooking and watch the Turkey Bowl. I make two different pies, and we decide to eat straight from the tins on the couch. I like balancing the pie on my swollen belly. It makes for a pretty good table. Luke keeps stealing bites of my chocolate pie while I threaten to stab him with my fork.

I can't remember a more perfect Thanksgiving.

With Adam, our holidays were always spent with his mother since I didn't have any family of my own. Susan would never let us hear the end of it if we didn't show up perfectly primped and polished for each and every holiday.

I never really recognized how much it bothered me until I sat on a worn leather couch, pie-faced, in my pajamas, surrounded by styrofoam containers, laughing with Luke.

Yup.

Best. Thanksgiving. Ever.

CHAPTER THIRTEEN

LIV

We're watching *The Princess Bride* on the couch while eating mint chocolate chip ice cream straight from the carton, passing the pint back and forth. It had been a long day at the office, and I was grateful for some downtime. My back is killing me.

"I have bad news," Luke says, while running his warm hand gently over my bare stomach. This has become a nightly ritual for us as Luke tries to bond with Little Man. Apparently, he read it in a book somewhere.

Or maybe it was the fruit app.

"What's the bad news?"

"I think I found your first stretch mark," he teases, lightly tracing his calloused finger on my lower belly above my left thigh.

"You have got to be kidding me!" I screech, trying to lift my belly and bend forward simultaneously in order to see the blasted line. I feel like I'm attempting an impossible position from the Kama Sutra.

"Apparently the coconut butter was a bust," Luke teases.

I had been religiously putting it on twice a day after reading online that it prevented stretch marks.

"Dammit!" I yell, finally finding the proper angle and seeing the bane of my existence.

Luke laughs at my overreaction. "Pretty sure stretch marks come along with the territory, Liv," he teases.

I scowl in his direction. Steam may or may not be coming out of my ears.

"I haven't felt sexy in seven freaking months! I look like I swallowed a watermelon. I can't see my toes. I can't bend over to shave my legs. I've got a giant pimple on my nose. Don't tell me you haven't seen it. It's like a third eye!" I growl. "They never tell you about the freaking pimples! They only talk about *the pregnancy glow*! Where's my glow? I want my freaking glow! And now, I see this giant purple line covering half my freaking stomach!" I yell.

Maybe I'm exaggerating a little bit. Okay, I'm definitely exaggerating. I also know I'm rambling. Yup. Definitely rambling. I just don't think Luke understands the gravity of that stupid stretch mark! It's like the straw that broke the freaking camel's back!

And have I mentioned those damn pregnancy hormones?

"Liv," Luke says, sternly. I ignore him, fuming.

"Liv!" he tries again, gaining my attention.

"What?" I growl.

"You are the sexiest woman I've ever seen. Hands down. You didn't swallow a watermelon. You have a tiny human being growing inside you. You can't see your toes? I can! They're cute, and tiny, and perfect. I can even paint your damn nails if you need me to. You can't shave your legs? Where's your razor? I'll do that, too. You have a pimple?" He lifts my chin towards him. "I saw you when you were sixteen years old. They went away then, and they'll go away in two months." He leans forward, making sure he has my full attention. "You want your glow? You damn, naïve, woman!" he yells, exasperated. "You've had that glow every single day of your life. You might not see it, but I do. And it makes you more beautiful than any other woman out there." He punctuates the last words by pointing toward the window.

I feel my eyes start to water and my cheeks flushing as he continues. "And this little stretch mark?" His finger lightly grazes the line. "It's the most beautiful reminder I will ever have of the miracle you created. I might not be this little boy's dad, but I will love him every single day of my life. And that means that I will love this little line, and any others you get in the next two months, more than you will ever know."

He's breathing heavy from his confession, his forest-green eyes so heated I feel them burning into me, tattooing his words onto my soul. I try to swallow the lump in my throat from his honesty. The silence is so heavy in the room I'm afraid I might suffocate, but I can't seem to break it.

He's been trying to tell me for months, but I think this is the first time that the truth has finally sunk in, and it hits me like a ton of bricks.

Luke isn't going anywhere. I'm not alone. Luke loves my Little Man. And I think he might even love me a little bit, too. As a friend, obviously.

He continues to hold my gaze, waiting for me to say something.

The problem is I'm not sure what I *should* say after a confession like that, so I simply stare at his hand resting on my swollen stomach, and whisper so quietly I'm almost shocked he hears me, "The nail polish is under the sink."

Luke laughs, his head tilted toward *The Princess Bride* still playing on the screen. He shakes his head, his green eyes twinkling as they hold my gaze once more. "As you wish."

Luke

After my little confession, Liv and I did what we always do. We swept it under the rug and pretended it never happened.

I had always been grateful for it in the past, but I'm getting tired of pretending. I did it for two years in high school, three years when we were apart, and six months with her living under my roof.

If I have to hold anything else in, I might explode.

It felt good to express myself last night. It felt good to laugh with her afterwards as I painted her toes a cheerful sunshine color (her words, not mine). It felt good as we watched Westley fight Prince Humperdinck, her legs in my lap.

Everything about her feels good.

CHAPTER FOURTEEN

LIV

D r. Fellows was a little hesitant to allow me to travel to Luke's parents' house for Christmas. My due date is only five weeks away, but we promised we wouldn't fly, and the drive is only about eight hours.

I feel like I'm going to pee my pants, but I already asked Luke to stop in the last town.

Maybe I need to go easy on the icees. But they help with my heartburn, and heartburn is pretty much the worst thing ever.

Worst. Thing. Ever.

I begin to wiggle in my seat, crossing my legs and bracing myself against any potholes. It's not like they have many on the highway, but a girl can never be too careful. Especially when it comes to not wetting her pants in front of her best friend who would never let her hear the end of it.

"How you doin' over there, Liv?" Luke glances at me before turning his eyes back to the road.

He's wearing a light blue t-shirt that stretches across his muscular chest, his worn blue jeans covering his thighs.

I grit my teeth as he lightly taps his brakes, causing my butt cheeks to clench in hopes of preventing an accident of a different kind all over Luke's leather seat and my simple black yoga pants.

I refuse to travel uncomfortably. Plus, yoga pants are pretty much the only thing I fit into right now, but that's beside the point.

"You okay?" he asks, his lips tilting upwards in a smirk. I'm pretty sure he knows what my problem is.

"Fine," I grit out, crossing my legs for the third time. "Just trying to keep your car clean."

His jade eyes glance my way again before his smirk turns into a devious grin. Luke turns down the volume on his car stereo and lets the silence envelop me. I shift uncomfortably in my seat.

"So...now probably wouldn't be a great time to tell you a joke?" he asks mischievously. His eyes are practically glowing with triumph, knowing how easy it would be to make my bladder explode like a water balloon.

I glare in his direction, praying he doesn't have any new material I've never heard.

I already know that politely asking him to keep his annoyingly gorgeous lips sealed will be pointless. When Luke is determined about something, there's no stopping him, and apparently, he wants to see me pee my pants.

Bastard.

That being said, it doesn't stop me from sticking my pointer fingers into my ears and humming a Taylor Swift song while refusing to look at Luke. Mature, I know. I squeeze my eyes shut and try to think of the clown from *It*, or my mother-in-law. Nothing's scarier than her.

After a few moments of silence, I open my eyes and peek at Luke. His eyes are glued to the road. I begin to wonder if he's given up, when I hesitantly lower my hands to rest on my swollen belly.

My eyes stay focused on the side of Luke's face, taking in his chiseled jaw and five o'clock shadow. His calloused palms grip the steering wheel casually.

After my eyes dart between the clock on the dashboard and Luke's annoyingly attractive face for exactly five minutes, I finally begin to feel my muscles relax. I've been tense for so long, I'm starting to get a Charlie horse in my left butt cheek.

I bite my lip, still cautiously awaiting his next move. Because like I said, he doesn't give up easily.

"So, I read an article in *National Geographic* the other day," Luke states, casually.

My eyebrows crinkle; I can't figure out what angle he's going for.

After a minute, I decide to throw him a bone because, how is the *National Geographic* funny? I roll my eyes before playing along, my curiosity peaked.

"Okay?" I ask, dragging out the word.

"Apparently, there were these two elephants that saw a naked guy running around."

I can't tell if that's the punchline to the dumbest joke ever, or if he really did read an article about elephants seeing a naked dude.

I shake my head slightly, waiting for him to get to his point. I grab my melted icee, placing the straw between my lips. I know I shouldn't be drinking anymore, but did I mention the heartburn?

"Anyway, the first elephant turns to the second and says, 'I really don't know how he can feed himself with that thing.'"

My brows continue to furrow as I take a drink. I look at

Luke, clueless as to what he's talking about until....

I snort loudly, spewing bright red cherry slushie through my nose and down his dashboard, causing me to laugh hysterically, burying my face in my hands.

That is the dumbest joke I've ever heard.

As I try to catch my breath between bouts of laughter, I say, "Joke's on you, my friend. 'Cause now you have to get your car cleaned."

It's not even that funny of a joke. Really. It isn't. However, the lengths my best friend will go to get me to pee my pants is ridiculous. Thankfully, his front seat will remain clean for now, even if his dashboard isn't.

That being said, I'm afraid my underwear won't stay dry for much longer if we don't find a rest stop soon. Just as I'm about to ask for a funnel and a cup, I see a Chevron sign as Luke turns on his blinker, merging off the exit.

I say a silent prayer in thanks, throwing the door open, and booking it to the restroom before Luke can even turn off the ignition.

After using the facilities, I lumber back to the car, my lower back aching from sitting for so long.

Carrying around a twenty-pound watermelon isn't easy on the joints.

Or the bladder.

Rubbing my chest, I attempt to relieve the heartburn that is still driving me crazy. Pregnancy is awesome. Seriously, a total miracle. But I'm *so* over all these shitty side effects.

I take a few deep breaths before grabbing the door handle, preparing for the next few *long* hours in the car.

As I slide back into my seat, I can see the dashboard has been cleaned, and a fresh cherry icee is sitting in the cup holder next to a brand-new container of Tums.

I glance over at Luke as he fiddles with the stereo, turning the music back on, totally oblivious to how much his small gestures mean to me.

The Liv Whisperer strikes again.

CHAPTER FIFTEEN

LIV

Two hours later, we finally pull into Luke's childhood home in the early evening. It's a beautiful two-story house covered in freshly fallen snow with twinkling Christmas lights hanging from the roof. The driveway has been recently shoveled, and I can't help but smile as the sharp breeze kisses my cheeks, turning them pink almost instantly.

I take a deep breath of the crisp winter air and look up at the cloudy sky. I've missed Utah. People might think it's full of Mormons and polygamists, but that's simply not true. Well, at least not the polygamist part. And Mormons are pretty cool, too.

There are plenty of normal, friendly people here, and Luke's family is definitely one of them. It's been almost five years since I've really seen them, and I can't wait to catch up with everyone. This was practically my second home in high school.

Adam's family was way too strict when it came to a bunch of teenagers hanging out, so we always spent the majority of our time at Luke's. I was a little nervous about coming back, afraid this place would stir up too many memories, but I can't help the feeling of excitement bubbling inside of me.

I've missed Mrs. Jensen like crazy. She was practically my second mom growing up, and it was hard losing touch with her. And let's not forget Breezy-Bree, Luke's younger sister. Those two are only eighteen months apart, and I loved hanging out with her. Luke always got annoyed when she'd tag along with us, but I loved having another girl in the group. And did I mention she's hilarious?

I can't help but feel disappointed in myself. Why do I let important people I care about fade into the background of my life without making them a priority? Nothing should get in the way of people you care about. I need to change that about myself. No matter what happens, I need to keep the importance of my relationships in perspective. I always complain about feeling alone, but maybe if I nurtured the friendships around me, that wouldn't be the case.

I shake off my morose thoughts, convinced my brain is just frazzled from our car ride. When did I get to be such a Debbie Downer?

I pull my light gray North Face coat closer to my body, or at least as close as I can with a giant belly in the way. I gave up zipping it closed a couple months ago. Luke places his hand on my lower back, guiding me toward the front door.

He raises his fist to knock, but before his knuckles can make contact with the stained wood, the door swings open revealing a very grown-up looking Bree. She shoves Luke out of the way before grabbing me in a giant bear hug. Bree must have the wingspan of a freaking NBA player because she somehow manages to reach all the way around me, and my massive stomach, squeezing me so tight that I can barely breathe.

Just as I begin to see black dots, she finally releases me before practically squealing, "My Livvy Lou! Oh my gosh! Where have you been all my life? Ever heard of a freaking telephone?" Her grin is so wide I'm afraid her face might split in half. "And how are you, my little snuggle bum?" She bends toward my belly, practically cooing. "Have you missed your Auntie Breezy? I bet you have, haven't you? When are you going to come out so I can hold you, my sweet little boy?" She starts rubbing my belly back and forth as if a genie might pop out.

I laugh out loud, having forgotten how much this girl talks. Her chocolate-colored hair is piled on top of her head in a messy bun, slightly curled pieces framing her face. She and Luke have the same striking green eyes, although hers are accented with dark eye makeup. She's as gorgeous as ever, and I secretly want to punch her for it.

"Girlie, I have missed you more than you can possibly imagine," I say, grinning right back at her. "How the hell are you?"

"Great! Just graduated from the U, still living at home 'cause that's what all the cool kids do, and am now looking for a job. Very exciting stuff," she smirks. "Just kidding! Well, not about the job part, 'cuz waitressing is *so* not my forte, but I did just sign on a new apartment! It's gonna be amaze-balls!" Bree does a little happy dance to physically express her excitement. "What's new with you? I mean, other than the bun in the oven, the new place to live, the new job, and the new roommate," she says, sticking her tongue out at Luke.

He shakes his head, grabbing Bree and pulling her into a headlock, because apparently, that's how these two say, "Hello."

It doesn't last long though, because Bree shoves her

elbow into his stomach, knocking the wind out of Luke and causing his grip to loosen. She twists out of his grasp before thrusting her fists into the sky, proclaiming herself champion. "Still got it, big brother. Nice try, though," she brags, walking backwards into the house. "Come on guys! We've got lots to catch up on and it's too damn cold to do it all on the porch," she yells, before turning toward the kitchen.

I'm still laughing as I wait for Luke to catch his breath. He rolls his eyes at me and shakes his head. "Have I told you how grateful I am that you're having a boy?" he says, exasperated.

I snicker, secretly grateful I'm having a boy, too. I don't think I could handle having a little girl like Breezy. She's a blast to hang out with, and I love her to death, but I've never envied her parents. She must've been hell to raise. The girl reminds me of a hurricane, sweeping in and causing all hell to break loose. She's powerful, loud, and impossible to ignore.

Luke places his hand on my lower back, guiding me into his parents' house. There's a staircase on the right leading to three regular bedrooms, a bathroom, and the master suite. On the left is a short hallway lined with family pictures, leading to the kitchen and family room. The walls are painted a warm gray color, making the home feel inviting to visitors.

As Luke leads me toward the kitchen, I pause to look at an old family picture taken before graduation. I can't help the soft smile that comes to my face as I'm reminded of the first time I saw him after transferring schools.

Everyone thinks I met Luke through Adam, and I guess you could say that's true, but it's definitely not the whole story. I'm pretty sure Luke would even tell you that Adam introduced us. And I guess he did, *technically*.

But that's definitely not *my* side of the story.

I was hiding behind a curtain of my thick blonde hair, sitting at my desk in the corner of my first period class. My palms were sweaty, and I was praying that I had some dormant superpower that allowed me to melt into the wall so I could disappear, or at least become invisible for the next few hours.

I felt the hairs on the back of my neck immediately stand on end, knowing someone was watching me. Curious, I looked toward the classroom entrance and saw him. A gorgeous guy with broad shoulders and unforgettable green eyes. I'm sure he was just curious about who the new student was, but butterflies immediately erupted in my lower stomach. My heart was racing.

I quickly turned back to my notebook and pretended to doodle, attempting to ignore him. He was taller than most kids my age and definitely had an athlete's build. His piercing gaze burning itself into my memory.

I caught myself holding my breath, unsure if I should peek to see if the gorgeous stranger was still looking my way. Instead, I was a coward and continued to stare at my desk, fiddling with my pen.

Just as I gained the courage to look at the beautiful male specimen leaning against the doorframe, the desk next to mine scraped six inches closer to me as a guy with sandy blonde hair sat down. He was attractive, too. He was a little shorter than the guy across the room, but still muscular, with straight white teeth and pale blue eyes. He leaned back in his chair, kicking out his legs like he owned the place. He smirked in my direction, like he knew a secret only he was privy to.

I glanced towards Mr. Green Eyes again. His arms were folded over his broad chest, a scowl on his face. Mr. White Teeth cleared his throat, demanding my attention. My gaze bounced between the two handsome strangers before finally landing on the guy sitting next to me.

I smiled shyly at him before biting my lower lip nervously. I wasn't used to this kind of attention, especially from two ridiculously attractive guys. Was there a lottery I won that I didn't know about?

"Hey! My name's Adam," Mr. White Teeth announced enthusiastically.

He held out his hand, waiting for me to shake it. I stared at it for a minute before remembering my manners. I quickly wiped my sweaty palm on my skinny jeans, feeling embarrassed, before placing my hand in his. He laughed good-naturedly, shook it once, then released it.

I could tell he was a happy guy, and definitely someone who would be fun to be around. It's amazing how telling first impressions could be.

I peeked toward the door once more, confused as to why I was even looking for Mr. Green Eyes. His gaze nailed me in place, the butterflies swarming in my belly all over again. I held my breath for a minute, unable to move, before he finally looked away, shaking his head slightly back and forth.

He seemed angry as he pushed himself off the doorframe. However, his face quickly morphed to one of indifference before he strolled toward the desk next to Adam. He pulled out his chair, sat down, and opened his notebook. He then began to write down the assignment that was written on the whiteboard.

Effectively ignoring me.

Which was fine.

I guess he just had to assess the new girl then move on to more important things. Like homework.

Adam cleared his throat again, gaining my attention. Had he said something?

I could kick myself for getting so distracted. I shook my head slightly, hoping to dispel the butterflies and help me to focus on the attractive guy sitting next to me. My cheeks were a lovely *shade of red from embarrassment. I wished Mr. White Teeth, I mean Adam, would repeat himself so I wouldn't feel like such an idiot.*

He laughed warmly in my direction, obviously not offended by my lack of attention. "I asked you what your name is?" Adam repeated patiently, his blue eyes shining. I could tell he was genuinely curious and not just asking to be polite.

I smiled nervously before answering, "My name's Liv."

Adam leaned a little closer. "Well, Liv, let me tell you a little secret," he whispered. "We're going to have one hell of an adventure."

--

Luke's warm hand lightly pushes me past the picture into the kitchen, scattering my memories from all those years ago like grains of sand in the wind. He seems oblivious to my little walk down memory lane, which I'm grateful for. I quickly get a handle on my emotions as we make our way toward his family.

The scents of warm vanilla and freshly baked cookies greet me as we enter the kitchen through the open archway. This house might be thirty years old, but Mrs. Jensen has always been good at keeping up with the latest decorating trends.

The Formica countertops that I remember have been replaced with beautiful swirling granite, and the cabinets look as though they have been recently painted in a creamy white color. The hardwood floors remain the same warm mahogany that I remember.

The house is cozy and inviting, making me feel right at home in a place that has never truly been mine.

My mouth begins to water as I take in the freshly baked treats scattering the island. Chocolate chip cookies, cinnamon rolls, and gingerbread men cover the countertops. My manners seem to have left the building as I catch myself reaching for a cookie.

Before I can grab one, I'm greeted by another warm hug as soon as Mrs. Jensen sees me. Apparently, I'm the guest of honor because, once again, Luke is pushed aside until I've been properly welcomed.

I'm wearing a smile that splits my face as I munch on some goodies and take in this beautiful family who is kind enough to let me tag along with their son for Christmas. I know we were pretty close at one point, but it's been *years*. And yet, as I'm surrounded by Luke's parents and siblings, it feels like it was only yesterday.

Luke

It's weird having Liv back at my parents' house. I can tell they've missed having her around. I can't help but smile as I remember Bree and my mom practically attacking her as soon as she entered the freaking house.

I'd forgotten how well she fits in with my family.

Maybe a little too well.

I have to keep reminding myself that I'm not bringing my girlfriend home to meet the family. That every time our eyes connect and her lips smile softly, it doesn't have some hidden meaning behind it. That anytime her hand brushes mine or her knee grazes my thigh as we sit down to eat dinner, it's just an innocent touch.

I have to keep reminding myself that she isn't mine, even though it's starting to feel that way.

CHAPTER SIXTEEN

LIV

I'm sitting on the couch rubbing my ridiculously full stomach, as I let out a sigh of contentment. My legs are in Luke's lap like always, and he's giving me a foot massage as we watch *Christmas Vacation* together.

His family is scattered throughout the house. Sarah, Luke's mom, and Jim, his dad, are cleaning up the kitchen, and Bree is talking to her boyfriend in the other room. Apparently, his name is Henry, and he works in an office somewhere. They haven't been together for long, but Bree seems super happy so I hope they work out. Luke's younger brother, Jake, is in his room playing video games.

I'm pretty sure I've just reached nirvana as I lick the last bit of frosting off my fingers. We have just finished dinner and, while the cinnamon rolls are technically for breakfast, I'm able to get away with sneaking one for dessert since I'm pregnant.

Fun fact: Pregnant women can get away with murder.

I smile mischievously, debating whether I should go grab a second one or not, but that would mean I'd risk cutting my foot massage short. And I'd have to stand back up.

Did I mention how difficult it is to roll around when you're carrying a twenty-pound basketball on your abdomen? I prefer to look like a beached whale as little as possible, thank you very much.

Alas, I guess that means I'll have to save my second cinnamon roll for tomorrow.

I catch Luke examining me from under his thick, dark eyelashes with a smirk on his face.

I look at him questioningly. "What?" I ask, hesitantly.

Luke looks at me like this all the time. Like I amuse him somehow. Or that I'm *being cute* but not in an attractive adult way. More like in a toddler singing off key and running around the room naked kind of way.

I catch myself feeling both annoyed and curious at the same time.

"What did I do now?" I ask exasperated, rolling my eyes.

He grins.

Bastard.

I can tell he's trying not to laugh as he slowly leans toward my face. My forehead creases, and I'm unsure why he's all up in my bubble. I'm suddenly very aware of our close proximity.

Pushing myself further into the cushions, Luke takes his forefinger and lightly grazes my lower lip. I'm not uncomfortable, exactly. More like I'm just confused about the feelings swirling inside of me.

Where the hell did these butterflies come from?

My gaze bounces between his eyes and his mouth before he slowly removes his finger from my face and shows me a small smudge of cream cheese frosting. His grin comes back full force as he places said frosting in his mouth, slowly licking his finger clean. My eyes zero in on his luscious lips, glimpsing his tongue as it swipes at the sugary icing. Time seems to slow down as I watch, mesmerized.

Luke leans back again, squeezing my feet as he says, "You're a hot mess, Liv. When are you gonna learn to eat without making a mess of yourself?" he teases before licking his lips again. "Although, I'm not complaining. I've been dying for a taste," he smirks. I can feel myself blushing, again.

Is it hot in here?

And why do I feel like he might not be talking about the frosting?

My gaze is glued to his as his grin slowly fades. He must've planned on me sweeping his comment under the rug like I usually do, but for some reason, I don't want to this time.

I might want a taste, too.

I just hope this isn't another stupid game of "chicken." I'm not sure I'll survive if it is.

The tension is so thick between us, you could cut it with a knife. I watch his Adam's apple bob up and down as he swallows thickly, licking his lips in anticipation.

I'm not sure what's happening right now, but I'm helpless to stop it. I'm not sure I'd want to, even if I could.

However, just as I'm positive Luke is about to lean closer, Bree comes strutting into the room and falls precariously onto the love seat by the TV. She's completely oblivious to the tension filling the room, and effectively breaks it with her presence.

"So, what are we watchin'?" she asks.

"Just our favorite guy making a fool of himself again," Luke mutters.

"Oh good! I love when Clark acts like an idiot!" Bree laughs.

I clear my throat and take a peek at Luke. "I don't think he *always* makes a fool out of himself," I whisper, quietly. I have a feeling Luke isn't talking about the movie.

Thankfully, Bree doesn't hear me. She's completely immersed in *Christmas Vacation*, which is probably a good thing since I wouldn't be able to explain my comment anyway.

CHAPTER SEVENTEEN

LIV

Yesterday was spent baking, eating, watching classic Christmas movies, and snuggling by the fire. Oh, and did I mention eating? Because we definitely did a lot of that. And it was awesome.

It was the perfect way to spend a holiday, and is exactly what I needed after a long ride in the car. My aching body definitely appreciated the break.

Today, however, we're heading to the Olympic Oval in Salt Lake. It was originally built for the 2002 Winter Olympics, but is now open to the public. I haven't been here since high school when Adam and I had a double date with Luke and his flavor of the week. Bree had tagged along as well, unashamed of being the fifth wheel.

We had spent the evening laughing, holding hands, drinking hot chocolate, and eating stale donuts from the gas station. I chuckle softly to myself, remembering Bree and I fighting over the last chocolate donut. Unfortunately, she won. She's a scrappy little fighter, that one.

It really was a perfect night.

I smile fondly, remembering how sweet Adam used to always treat me.

He was a really good guy.

I know that college was tough on him and our relationship, but high school was a completely different story. Well, the majority of it anyway. The last semester took its toll on Adam, too. He was always so hard on himself, trying to please everyone and trying to be perfect.

Despite that, the guy waited on me hand and foot. He really knew how to make a girl feel like a princess. I know I was his entire world, just like how he was mine.

I take a deep breath as we pull into the parking area, surprised that my walk down memory lane didn't leave me in tears. It's refreshing to think about my first love without breaking down afterwards. I think Adam would be proud of me. My eyes glaze slightly with the overwhelming feeling of peace that encompasses me.

I *know* he would be.

My soft smile is still firmly in place as Luke grabs my hand across the center console. He squeezes it gently, taking in my glossy eyes before asking, "You ready for this, Liv? You better be careful. I'm pretty sure I've never seen an eight-month pregnant woman ice skate before," he teases, gently.

I laugh, wiping under my eyes. "Bring it on."

We make our way into the arena, meeting his family by the area where you rent skates.

Breezy comes bouncing over holding two pairs of skates over her head. "Gotcha covered, slow pokes!" she teases, while handing both Luke and me a pair. "Now, suit up, Ted!" she jokes, quoting *How I Met Your Mother*. "We'll meet you on the ice!"

Bree bobbles toward the rink on her skates as Luke and I

take seats on one of the many benches scattered throughout the area to lace up. While attempting to bend forward and slip off my shoes, I hear Luke chuckling in my direction before sliding off the bench and kneeling before me. He grabs my moccasin-covered feet and slips them off. "Don't hurt yourself, Liv," he teases. "Let me you help out."

I roll my eyes, feeling like a toddler, but reluctantly grateful for his thoughtfulness. We both stay silent as he continues to tie my skates.

Looking around the arena, I take in the fun atmosphere. It looks like your average skating rink, except bigger. There are flags hanging from the ceiling, along with the Olympic rings decorating the walls, and a running track surrounding the ice.

I notice a family with three small children near us. The mom is smiling in my direction as the dad is rounding up their kids. I smile back, silently laughing at the father's exasperated face.

Luke finishes lacing up my skate and sets my foot back on the ground. He then leans forward, places his large hands on my round stomach, and rubs gently. "You ready for this, Little Man?" He kicks at that exact moment, and Luke's face lights up. My little boy is wiggling constantly now, but it never ceases to amaze me how excited Luke gets every time he feels him move.

Luke chuckles quietly before speaking to my belly once more. "I know, I know. Soon enough it'll be you out there bud, and I'll be lacing up *your* skates." He smiles softly and glances up at me with his gorgeous green eyes.

I can't help but grin as I see this giant man on his knees in front of me, talking to my unborn baby.

I hear someone clearing their throat slightly, gaining our

attention. Breaking eye contact with Luke, I look over to see the mom with the three little kids.

"You two are the cutest couple ever, and are going to make great parents! I can already see how much you love your little one." She smiles sincerely.

Luke stiffens, his cheeks reddening from her inaccurate observation, but I stop him before he can correct her. "Thank you. We are so excited to meet him! Only one more month!" I reply, happily.

"Well, it'll be here before you know it! It was so nice meeting you!" She grabs her littlest girl's hand and leads her toward the ice.

Luke clears his throat and stands up from his kneeling position in front of me. He rubs his hands through his hair before sheepishly looking my way. "Sorry, Liv. I know how much you hate it when people make assumptions."

I shake my head back and forth before grabbing his face so I have his full attention, which is kind of hard to do considering our height difference. "Luke. It's not your fault at all. And it's not a problem." I shrug. "Seriously. I know our situation is a little..." I pause, looking for the right word, "unorthodox? But it's okay. You *have* kind of stepped into the supportive father role, and even though we're not a couple or anything, I know that you care about this little guy." I lick my lips before continuing. "Don't get me wrong. I know you're not his dad, and I'm not asking you to be. But I also kind of love how much you love him already. So, thank you for that."

I feel a light blush stain my cheeks as I finish my vulnerable monologue. I let my hands fall to my sides and clear my throat, suddenly uncomfortable with his undivided attention. I look down at my stomach, picking at invisible lint and effectively breaking his intense gaze.

Luke grabs my left hand, gently intertwining our fingers before bringing it to his lips and placing the softest of kisses on the back. He smiles softly and nods his head once, acknowledging my confession without verbal confirmation before leading me toward the ice.

Which is exactly what I need.

CHAPTER EIGHTEEN

LIV

As soon as I'm on the ice, I'm reminded of how much I suck at skating. Obviously, this wasn't my brightest idea. Especially when you factor in my basketball belly, which doesn't exactly help with balance.

However, I'm stubborn enough to go through with it regardless. I need a few moments away from Luke after our intense conversation. As I see Breezy skating around the corner, I find the perfect excuse to extract myself from Luke.

"Hey Breezy! Help a pregnant woman out, would ya?" I yell.

Bree laughs before gracefully skating toward me and grabbing my hand, stealing me away from her brother. The girl is one of the most clumsy people I've ever met, yet she's somehow a pro at ice skating.

Go figure.

"Sorry, Luke! She's mine now!" Bree yells over her shoulder, whisking me away on the ice.

I can still hear Luke's laughter as we turn the next corner. We're going pretty slowly, because I wasn't joking about my lack of balance, when Bree gives me a knowing look. "So...you and my brother, eh?" she asks, feigning innocence.

My eyes nearly pop out of my head at the absurdity of her question. "What? Are you serious? No. No, no, no," I ramble, shaking my head back and forth. Thankfully, the girl is still holding my hand, or I'm pretty sure I would've fallen flat on my face.

She snorts loudly. "Oh. Okay. Still in denial then," she teases.

I glare at her from the corner of my eye, trying to focus on my stability as well as the conversation. "What do you mean, still in denial?" I ask, both frustrated and curious at the same time.

"Nothing." She smiles, mischievously. "So, have you heard the one about the two elephants?" she jokes, not-so-subtly changing the subject.

I throw my head back, laughing, and nearly fall on my ass before peeking over my shoulder, hoping Luke didn't see. I find him just rounding the corner, a smirk covering his face as he gives me an *I told you so* look. He warned me that my natural clumsiness, combined with ice and pregnancy, would not be a good combination.

I laugh harder before gripping Bree's hand so tight I'm afraid her fingers might fall off and continue to skate for the rest of the afternoon, sneaking glances at Luke every chance I get.

Luke

First, there is her little confession, hinting that she wants me to be part of Little Man's life, causing my heart to nearly beat out of my chest. Her eyes portraying such a vulnerable honesty, leaving only questions in their wake.

Then there is her lack of ice-skating skills, causing multiple heart attacks, along with multiple prayers of gratitude that Bree took four years of skating lessons.

Lastly, her eyes are always wandering until she finds me all throughout the afternoon. A soft smile grazing her lips every time her eyes connect with mine. I think she's finally starting to heal.

That girl will be the death of me.

CHAPTER NINETEEN

LIV

I ce-skating was a blast, but I'm pretty sure I could sleep for a week. I wouldn't tell a soul, but the Braxton Hicks contractions are definitely hitting full force. A few are even hard to breathe through. I keep reassuring Luke that I'm fine, but I definitely need a nice warm bath to soothe my aching muscles.

"So, my mom was wondering if you're planning on visiting Susan while you're in town?" Luke asks as we drive home, eyeing me from his side of the car.

I shrug, noncommittally. I'm still undecided whether I will, or won't, be seeing my dear old mother-in-law. I've never felt so at war with myself over something. I know what's the right thing to do, but it will also be significantly more difficult.

Battling my conscience on a daily basis isn't exactly easy, either.

I continue to stare out the window hoping Luke will let it go, and I can bury my head in the sand for a little while longer.

Mature, I know.

"You know Adam would want his mom to be involved. I know she's crazy, but she's still his family. I'm just saying." Luke leans across the center console and squeezes my thigh gently, trying to lessen the sting of his honesty.

I let out a deep breath through my lips, knowing he's right, and hating him a little bit for it.

"I know," I whisper, quietly.

--

Once we're home, I immediately head toward the bathtub upstairs. My aching feet slowly dragging me to my destination. The rest of the evening should be pretty low-key considering Christmas Eve is tomorrow, and Sarah will just be cooking until then. I decide to take advantage of the free time by soaking in a nice bubble bath.

I've decided to visit Susan tomorrow afternoon, before her annual Christmas Eve party. I figure I'll be able to get out of her hair before the festivities, and she can brag to all her friends how happy she is to be a grandma. *If* she's happy, that is. I blow out air through my lips, debating how I'm going to drop the bomb on her. Looking down at my giant belly, I decide I won't need to say much.

After my heavenly bath, I slip into another pair of black yoga pants and a pink maternity t-shirt that says, "Preg-gosaurus," with a dinosaur on it. Luke got it for me a few weeks ago out of the blue, saying he couldn't resist. It's my most favorite shirt ever.

Making my way downstairs, I see everyone sitting at the table, playing Two Truths and a Lie. It's a pretty simple game where everyone comes up with two truths about themselves and one lie. The object of the game is to detect which "fact" is false.

You'd think the game would be boring when playing with your family who already knows everything about you, but it actually makes it more fun because you have to be more creative with both your truths, and your lie.

I take a seat to the left of Breezy, with Luke sitting across from me, his mom sitting on his left, and his dad at the head of the table on Bree's right. Apparently, Jake is still playing video games in his room.

They're about to begin a new round.

It's Bree's turn, and the table is quiet as she tries to think of her "facts."

After a minute, she starts her turn. "I made up Henry's occupation. He doesn't actually work in an office. He's between jobs right now. I actually hate *Christmas Vacation* with a vengeance because Clark freaking Griswold is such a stupid idiot. And I've decided I want a puppy for Christmas and will be buying one when I get into my apartment."

We're going clockwise, so it's my turn to guess which "fact" is actually a lie. After debating for a minute, I decide it's the *Christmas Vacation* one. That girl knows every single line in that movie. There's no way she hates it, and she's definitely impulsive enough to buy a puppy without thinking it through.

"*Christmas Vacation*."

"Puppy," Luke states confidently, folding his arms over his chest and leaning back in his chair.

"Puppy," repeats, Sarah.

"I'm hoping it's Henry because you can't honestly be dating a guy without a job, but I have a feeling it's puppy, too," Jim says, exasperated.

Bree laughs before announcing, "Puppy for the win! I am not getting a dog, everyone! And sorry Dad, but he's a really great guy! I know you'll love him, even though he doesn't have a job at the moment."

Jim's face turns pale at Bree's confession.

"You're turn, Liv!" Sarah says pointedly, hoping to change the subject from Bree's bad taste in men.

"Piece of cake," Luke says cockily.

I raise my eyebrows. "Oh really, Luke? You think you know me so well that I can't fool you?" I ask, the challenge clear in my voice.

Luke smirks in my direction, tapping his finger against his chin. "Let's make it interesting, Liv. If you can slip something past me, I'll buy you that fancy car seat and stroller combo you've been eyeing. But if I win, I get to choose Little Man's middle name."

My jaw hits the floor. I've been drooling over the Chicco Bravo Trio Travel System for months now, but it's way out of my price range. How did he know about that? I thought I'd been so sneaky by only drooling in my private time.

On the other hand, Luke's been begging me to have the baby's middle name be Danger so that he can say, "Danger's my middle name."

He thinks he's so funny. *Cue eye roll.*

I pause, biting my lip as I nervously contemplate if I want to take this bet or not. I take a deep breath before standing and reaching my hand across the table so we can shake on it.

What can I say? I'm a sucker for a nice car seat and stroller.

"Deal," I say as confidently as I can, even though my inner girl is shaking in her proverbial boots.

His smirk turns into a full-on grin, showcasing his straight white teeth. "Deal," he repeats, boldly. He grasps my hand firmly from across the table, shaking it once before releasing me.

I swallow thickly, my mind instantly searching for things he doesn't know about me. I quickly realize how difficult this is going to be in order to win, and losing is *not* an option. He just knows me too damn well.

I clear my throat once before starting my turn. "Adam wasn't my first kiss, although he thought he was. I've never broken a bone, and..." I shift my eyes toward the table, embarrassed to actually say this out loud, "I had a crush on Luke before Adam ever asked me out." I bite my lip nervously, wondering if I've played my cards right.

Luke's gaze is burning a hole in my forehead, but I refuse to look up. I realize I'm holding my breath as I wait for Luke to guess which fact is false. After what feels like an eternity, Luke finally breaks the silence.

"Never broken a bone," he states confidently from across the table. My forehead creases almost instantly, my eyes darting up to his.

Taking in his cocky demeanor, I'm disappointed with how easily he read through me.

He didn't even hesitate. I haven't told a soul about my real first kiss. It was before I transferred schools, and I've never spoken about it since. How the hell would he know that?

I've also never told a soul that I had a crush on Luke at one point, afraid it would hurt my relationship with Adam. Why wouldn't he have guessed that one? Was I that obvious?

And the bone thing? No one knows that I broke my stupid pinky toe from stubbing it on my dresser when I was little.

"How the hell did you know that?" I mutter under my breath, feeling anxious and confused.

He smirks in my direction, his body oozing confidence. "You used to shift uncomfortably any time Adam would bring up being your first and last kiss." His smile slightly falters, like it always does when bringing up his best friend, before he clears his throat and continues, glossing over my confession of having a little crush on him. "And the third fact had to have merit because you have a tiny little bump on your left pinky toe that I came across the last time I painted your toe nails. It's still a little tender sometimes. I was able to assume you'd broken it at one point." His smile is back full-force. "Therefore, I win, Sweetheart. Haven't you learned by now not to play games with me?" he jokes cockily, his stare pinning me in place.

I'm seething from his little speech. I can practically feel steam coming from my ears. There's no way in hell I'm letting him name my child Danger.

"Double or nothing," I spit, glaring at him from across the table. If looks could kill, he'd be shriveled up on the floor right now.

"I'm sorry. I must've heard you wrong, Sweetheart," Luke jokes, placing his hand behind his ear for better hearing. "There's no way you can be serious. What else would you want to bet?"

By now, his entire family is staring at us, completely intrigued. At one point Jake must've heard the commotion because he comes in with a giant bowl of popcorn and is passing it around to his sister and parents.

Bree pops a buttery piece into her mouth before saying, "Ooo...I like it. She's raised the stakes!"

I glare at her before turning my attention back to Luke. "There's no way I'm letting you name my baby Danger, so it doesn't matter what else we put on the table. I'm not going to let you win twice."

Luke grins mischievously before leaning forward and placing his elbows on the table. "So, you're telling me that I can bet whatever I want? No questions asked?"

His gaze turns predatory, and I definitely feel like the weaker prey. I contemplate backing down before the name *Danger* flashes through my mind.

"Deal." The word leaves my mouth before I can stop it. "Only this time, I get to guess."

Luke looks at me, intrigued. "Deal."

Bree squeals with excitement at the turn of events and starts clapping. "This is better than reality TV!" she exclaims.

I ignore her, continuing to glare at Luke instead. "Whenever you're ready, Sweetheart," I say condescendingly.

Luke leans back, his arms crossed over his broad chest, and taps his forefinger against his chin.

"First," he holds up his index finger, "moved away from home to get a good college experience. Second," he lifts his middle finger, "I came to your wedding and sat outside the chapel the entire time, leaving after you said, 'I Do.' And third," he holds up his ring finger, "the biggest regret I've ever had was who I asked to prom, even if that's not entirely on me."

His stare continues to hold mine from across the table. I feel a little shaken by his choice of facts. I'm speechless, actually. I try to clear my head of the emotions racing through me and remember this is just a game. A game that I *need* to win.

I think through each specific fact.

First, *he moved away from home to get a good college experience.* Obviously, true. That's what he told me when he was applying, and that's what he told me the day he left. That's also what his parents told me every time I saw them, even if I only saw them rarely. I feel like that's an easy one. But maybe it's an easy one on purpose, and he wants me to immediately dismiss it.

Gah! Now I'm second-guessing myself.

Let's move on.

Second, *he came to my wedding and sat outside the chapel until I said, "I Do."* I'm not sure if there's any truth behind this. Actually, I'm pretty sure there isn't. But he wouldn't make it that easy, now would he? He had told me he couldn't make it to the wedding because of school. That, I remember. His finals were later than Adam's, so he couldn't attend. It made perfect sense. I was bummed he didn't come, but I understood. Especially after seeing how hard finals were on Adam. It made sense why he wouldn't be able to celebrate with us.

I shake my head, remembering how sad I was that he couldn't make it. *I had missed him like crazy.*

I clear my throat. *On to the last fact.*

Third, *the biggest regret he's ever had was whom he asked to prom.* Seriously? That's kind of ridiculous. I try to think back to prom, but I don't remember much about his date. I think her name was Beth or something? I was still pretty new, so I didn't know the girls very well. Especially since I only ever hung out with Luke and Adam. But I'm pretty sure he made out with her the whole time, so it couldn't have been *that* big of a regret.

As I battle with myself about which fact is fake, I see Bree's hand shoot into the air as she starts waving it proudly back and forth. "I know which one's false! I know which one's false!" she chants.

I look over at her before Luke growls, "Eyes on me, Liv." His commanding tone grabs my attention. My gaze immediately falls back on Luke, his eyes pinning me in place.

"Bree, put your damn hand down before I make you leave the room," he barks at her, his eyes never leaving mine.

From the corner of my eye, I see Bree slowly place her hand back in her lap.

"What's your answer, Liv?" Luke asks, huskily.

I bite my lower lip, debating internally, yet unable to look away from Luke's piercing green eyes.

"What's your answer, Sweetheart?" Luke repeats, sincerely.

I'm afraid I might know the answer, but it's not the one I'm willing to voice out loud, so I go a different route.

"My wedding," I whisper, quietly. *There's no way he could've been there.*

Luke shakes his head almost imperceptibly. If I'd blinked, I would've missed it.

He raps his knuckles on the oak table before standing and making his way over to me. Luke leans down and whispers in my ear, "Wrong again, Sweetheart." Goosebumps erupt over my neck and arms at his close proximity, but before I can turn to look at him, he's already in the hallway heading upstairs.

Bree chuckles awkwardly, trying to break the tension in the room. Unfortunately, it doesn't work. "Whelp, who's up for a movie?" she asks the silent room. Jake mutters something about video games before following Luke upstairs, and Sarah and Jim nod eagerly at Bree's idea of a movie. I let out a breath I hadn't realized I was holding and follow them to the family room, all the while wondering what I now owed Luke, and when he would want to collect.

CHAPTER TWENTY

LIV

W e watched *Elf*. It's a classic, but I was bummed Luke didn't watch it with me. He never came down from his room after our little game that I lost miserably.

I'm pretty shocked he didn't take full advantage of his bragging rights. I mean, technically he did win. And technically, I do need to give him free reign for Little Man's middle name.

I shudder at the thought.

I also owe him *something else*, if only I knew what it was. Why in the world was I stupid enough to bet so blindly? I mean, seriously? That's got to be in the top ten dumbest things I've ever done. Although, from his absence tonight, it looks like I won't be paying up any time soon.

I can't decide whether that's a good thing or not. The anxiety of the unknown is eating me alive. I can't stop glancing toward the staircase any time I hear a creak in the old house.

After *Elf*, everyone decides to watch a double feature. And by everyone, I mean Bree and her parents. Luke is still missing, and Jake is busy gaming, or at least that's what I assume. I, however, am exhausted and decide to call it a night.

I head to the bathroom on the second floor and wash my face. I would get into my pajamas, but I'm already in them so...yup. No need for those. I pull my hair into a small messy bun at the base of my neck and pee one more time so that I won't have to roll out of bed in a few hours.

Have I ever mentioned how freaking often you need to go to the bathroom when you're pregnant? I swear, as soon as you pee on that little stick, your bladder shrinks to the size of a pea.

Afterwards, I open Bree's bedroom door, which is where I've been staying. It's decorated in cream and lavender. Very girly. Very Bree. There's a queen-sized bed in the center of the room with a paisley comforter and a dozen mismatched pillows. My favorite touches are the cat posters decorating the walls. As I'm about to climb into bed, my phone dings with an incoming text.

I see Luke's name flash on the screen, my heart skipping a beat before quickly opening up the message.

Luke: You ready to pay up, Sweetheart?

Liv: I'm not sure, since I still don't know what I owe you.

Luke: That's half the fun. Do you trust me?

I hesitate before replying. Do I trust him?

Liv: Maybe a little too much.

Luke: Don't worry. I won't let you down. Come outside.

My forehead creases. Outside?

Liv: Like, outside, outside?

Luke: Duh. Bring a jacket.

I roll my eyes, as he's still my same old Luke. After our little game, I didn't know what to expect. Especially since he disappeared on me.

Liv: Fine. But you owe me.

I see the little bubble showing he's typing something. As I wait for his reply, I slip on some snow boots and my grey North Face coat. My phone dings with another incoming text.

Luke: No, Sweetheart. YOU owe ME. That's why you're coming out in the first place. Silly pregnancy brain.

I catch myself smiling at my phone before opening Bree's door and waddling down the stairs toward the front door.

I open it to find Luke standing with his hands in his coat pockets. His shoulders are bunched up to protect himself from the cold, and his dark hair is lightly speckled with white snowflakes. His cheeks are tinged pink from the winter air, and he's smiling shyly at me.

I've never really seen Luke nervous before, but that's definitely how he's acting right now. He slowly rocks back and forth on his heels, his eyes shifting between me and the beautiful winter wonderland encompassing the front yard.

"Hi," he says, shyly.

"Hi," I reply, smiling. Luke's pretty cute when he's nervous.

"So..." he pauses. "How ya doin'?"

I laugh as he tries to make small talk. "A little chilly actually." I grin. "Any chance you wanna tell me what we're doing out here before I catch a cold?" I tease, enjoying watching him squirm.

He shrugs noncommittally before grabbing my frozen hand with his warm one and leading me off the porch. "Walk with me for a minute." He pulls me along before I have a chance to reply.

Laughing again, I release his hand and wrap my arm around his strong bicep, leaning my head against his shoulder. We slowly make our way under a giant maple tree in the front yard. It's covered in twinkling Christmas lights and white powdery snow. We follow a set of footprints packed into the ground until we're standing directly underneath a few tall branches.

"I'm sorry I disappeared. I just needed some time to wrap my head around a few things," he apologizes to me while running his hand over his hair. It's slightly damp from the snow. The moisture causes his hair to stand up in every direction, making him look as though he just rolled out of bed.

He looks sexy as hell.

I silently berate myself, trying to focus on the conversation and not how attractive Luke is. Which is a surprisingly difficult task, given how the moonlight is making his eyes sparkle. I giggle to myself, imagining how embarrassed Luke will feel if I let him know I just described his eyes as *sparkly*.

His eyebrow quirks before he asks, "What's so funny?" Obviously, his curiosity has gotten him a little off track from his original purpose.

I shake my head back and forth, giggling hysterically as I imagine my daydream coming to fruition. "Your eyes are particularly *sparkly* right now," I huff out between bouts of laughter.

He throws his head back, laughing, before wrapping his arms around me and pulling me into a hug. It's a little difficult with my belly in the way, but he somehow manages.

Luke starts to rock me back and forth, swaying gently, as he continues chuckling. "See, Liv? This is why you're perfect. I was having an absolute meltdown after our little game inside, afraid I had ruined our friendship by being too open or something, and yet you find a way to bring me back down to earth and help me step away from the ledge of insanity." He places a gentle kiss on the crown of my head as I nuzzle closer.

I smirk before repeating his words into his chest, "Ledge of insanity, Luke? Really?"

I feel his chest shake slightly from chuckling. "You know what I mean!" he says, exasperated. "I'm just so grateful I have this, Liv." He pauses and clears his throat. "That I have you." His voice loses its humor as he finishes his statement quietly, making me wonder if I was supposed to hear that last part or not.

I slowly lift my head from the warmth of his chest, our arms still wrapped around each other. I can feel the importance of this particular moment. I know this is Luke being honest. Vulnerable. He isn't hiding behind his sarcasm or his sense of humor. He isn't hiding behind a game of chicken, or even Adam for that matter. He's laying it all out there, which he's never done before.

I slowly lick my lips, letting his simple declaration sink in. His cheeks are flushed, and I can see his breath in the chilly air. *He's grateful he has me.* And for once, I'm not sure he's talking about that in a platonic sense.

Luke takes his calloused palm and lightly grasps my jaw, his other hand on my lower back. He's holding me in place carefully as if I'm a fragile china doll and he's afraid I might slip through his fingers.

"I know I'm not Adam, and that I'll never be him," he swallows thickly. "I know you won't ever really get over him, and that I'll always be second place, but I'm okay with that. I'm okay as long as I can share a small piece of you. I know I'll never have all of you. I get that. But I'm sick of waiting. Hoping. Questioning every single thing I do around you.

Wondering if I should give you more time, or if you might feel the same way."

He tilts my chin toward his as he leans closer. I can feel his breath on my face. I can practically taste the peppermint on his tongue. His green eyes stare into mine, pinning me in place, marking my soul with their sincerity.

"I'm done playing it safe," he whispers. "I'm taking what I should have that first day in class, instead of being a coward and letting you slip through my fingers." His lips are so close to mine I can almost feel them against my own as he whispers, quietly. "And now I'm going to taste you, like I've wanted to since the first time I saw you."

My eyes notice the mistletoe hanging from the branch directly over our heads, causing me to smile softly as Luke leans closer. "Mistletoe, Luke?" I whisper, teasingly against his lips. "You didn't think your little speech was gonna get you any action?"

I can feel his smile sweep across my own. "A guy's gotta do what a guy's gotta do," he whispers back, his lips brushing against mine like a butterfly's kiss. "Now shut up and let me kiss you." His grip tightens slightly before his lips tenderly touch my own. My eyelids slowly slide closed as I relish his touch. His mouth is so soft against my own as he lightly nibbles my lower lip.

I'm only stunned for a moment before I tightly grasp his forearm, holding him in place, remembering it takes two to tango. I stand on my tiptoes, my other hand gripping his coat and pulling him closer to me. He growls deep in his throat before he deepens the kiss, tilting my head where he wants me to be. He's possessive as his tongue slips into my mouth, coaxing my own to tangle with his. He tastes exactly how I've imagined he would. Like peppermint and hot chocolate.

He tastes perfect.

My chest rises and falls quickly as I try to catch my breath between kisses. His luscious lips start to slow. He pulls away slightly, pressing a tender kiss to my mouth once more. My eyes are still closed, and I begin to wonder if I'm dreaming, while praying that I'm not.

This simple kiss feels more right than anything I've ever experienced.

I'm flooded with so many emotions it's ridiculous. I want to laugh and cry at the exact same time. *Maybe it's the hormones?*

Guilt tries to press its way in, but I push it away, refusing to ruin such a perfect moment. I'm standing underneath the mistletoe surrounded by snow, Christmas lights, and the warmth of Luke's embrace.

It really is perfect.

And while I don't want to ruin said perfection, I can't help the words that quietly slip from my lips. "You'll never be second, Luke."

I whisper it so softly, I'm not even sure he hears me. I'm afraid my words might be swept away in the gentle breeze, but I need him to understand that there's never been a comparison between him and Adam. His brief confession before our kiss broke my heart. I don't want him to ever see himself as a lesser man than Adam.

He isn't. He never *was*.

He just wasn't quite fast enough, and Adam beat him to the punch, so to speak. Despite that, we can't change the past, and I wouldn't want to. But I do need him to understand that I can't be with someone who compares themselves to my deceased husband, so I decide to repeat myself a little more loudly this time.

"Luke." I look into his vibrant eyes, making sure I have

his full attention before continuing. "You'll never be second."

Luke places a gentle kiss on my frozen nose, his lips scorching me with their heat.

"You're freezing, Sweetheart," he whispers, taking in my rosy cheeks and cherry red nose. An affectionate smile is covering his face, his eyes still sparkling.

I've said my piece so I decide to let it go, savoring our closeness instead of focusing on his bitter remark from earlier.

"Well yeah," I reply. "Some idiot led me outside to freeze to death just so he could get some action," I smirk up at him, teasingly.

He chuckles good-naturedly before grabbing my hand.

"Come on Smartass. Let's get you some Cocoa and thaw out your pretty little fingers." He lifts my hand and kisses it lightly before leading me back toward the house. I wrap my frozen hand around his bicep again, resting my head against his shoulder once more, grinning from ear to ear as we trudge through the snow.

Best. Bet. Ever.

CHAPTER TWENTY-ONE

LIV

After some delicious hot chocolate and leftover cinnamon rolls, I finally head upstairs. I'm both physically and emotionally exhausted from the long and eventful day. Ahem, and night.

I kissed Luke.

These three words have been running nonstop through my head, even during our late-night snack when Luke and I chatted with his parents. We acted as if nothing really happened, but I can't stop thinking about it.

His lips touching mine, softly. Teasing me. Tasting me. His hands holding me firmly in place, bending me to his will. The heat of his body scorching mine through all our layers of clothing. His smile afterwards, like he was the luckiest person on the planet.

I sigh, dreamily.

I kissed Luke. I still can't believe it really happened as I slip through Bree's bedroom door. Mixed emotions are swirling inside of me, changing from elated to guilty, shocked, confused, then back to ecstatic in a never-ending roller coaster.

The one thing I'm certain of is that I don't regret it. At all. I just don't know what this turn of events means for my baby and me.

I'm not sure what I *want* it to mean.

Before I can even begin to wrap my head around *the kiss,* I catch Breezy sitting on her bed cross-legged, with a devious grin on her face like the cat who ate the canary.

My cheeks immediately heat, and I avoid eye contact, choosing to stare at her cutesy cat poster instead.

"What?" I ask as innocently as possible, shrugging my shoulders. I decide to play oblivious. Maybe she doesn't know anything. *Although she is a nosey little thing.*

"Don't 'what' me, missy!" she bosses, climbing off the bed and placing her hands on her hips. She's wearing dark blue Victoria's Secret yoga pants with PINK written on her bum and a coral colored tank top. Her hair is in a loose braid, hanging over her left shoulder. She looks like a mom who just caught her teenage daughter sneaking in after curfew. Her toes are anxiously tapping the carpet and everything.

I snort at the ridiculousness of the situation. One, I'm older than her. Two, I'm already knocked up, so what more could happen? And three, I've never had a single person wait up to yell at me if I was out past curfew. *Because I never was.* But that's beside the point. My Grandma was always asleep by 8:30pm, so I could pretty much do whatever I wanted.

While it's refreshing to know someone other than Luke or Adam cares about my well being, I'm still not sure I'm ready to admit to that someone that I kissed Luke.

I kissed Luke.

I sigh dreamily, again.

A ghost of a smile touches my lips before I remember to

school my features. Apparently, I'm not quick enough because Bree is instantly waving her finger at me, pointing at my not-so-good poker face.

"I saw that!" she shouts. "Now tell me *exactly* what happened! I need details!"

My smile returns with a vengeance, nearly splitting my face in half. My heart begins to race as I remember Luke's lips on mine.

"I don't know what you're talking about," I answer mischievously, walking toward the bed and sitting down.

Her eyes narrow as she keeps her finger pointed in my direction. "Don't give me that bull. We both know you're hiding something. Now where have you been?" she asks, accusingly.

I debate on whether I should tell her or not, but finally decide to throw her a bone. Her neutral opinion on the matter might help me sort through all these mixed emotions. Not that she's very unbiased, but still.

I clear my throat before blurting, "I kissed Luke." I bite my lower lip, anxious to see her reaction.

"I knew it!" she screams, jumping up and down.

I launch off the bed (which is quite the feat for a pregnant woman) and cover her mouth with my hand.

"Shh! Will you shut up?" I whisper-yell at her.

She licks my palm, causing me to squeal and release her. I wipe my hand on my pajamas before sticking out my tongue in her direction. "Ew. Gross."

She laughs good-naturedly before wrapping me in a bear hug.

"Finally!" she huffs. "I've been waiting for this day since forever!"

I pull away from our embrace, my eyebrow raised. "What do you mean *forever*?"

"Oh, come on, Liv," she says, exasperated. "You're telling me that you had no idea he's been in love with you forever? And that he'd do anything for you? And that you marrying Adam was the hardest thing he's ever had to live with? And that you living with him has been the sweetest torture imaginable?" Bree asks, batting her eyelashes in my direction.

I feel my jaw drop, shocked at her blunt assessment. I guess I shouldn't be, since that's what Breezy's known for. Her frank honesty.

I bite my lip again, taking in her statement. I'm not sure I'm ready for how quickly she mentioned the "L" word.

Luke and I kissed. And it was incredible. I don't regret it. I would definitely like to do it again and again in the near future. But am I ready to commit to him? *Can* I commit to him? I'm not really sure. I don't want to hurt him, and I definitely don't want to lose him.

I honestly don't know what to do.

Was it wrong to kiss him? It definitely didn't feel wrong. In fact, it felt right. All kinds of right. So right, that I'm weak in the knees just thinking about it. And this isn't just some guy. This is Luke. *My Luke.* My best friend. *The Liv Whisperer.* He's the one person I know I can lean on. The one person who is always there for me. Or at least, he *was.*

Why did he leave all those years ago? But maybe it doesn't matter why he left. Maybe all that matters is that he's here now. And he's made it clear that he isn't going anywhere.

I trust him. *I do.*

Adam isn't coming back. He's gone, and he would want me to be happy. Luke makes me happy. All Adam ever cared about was that I was taken care of, that I was loved. And Luke loves me. Or at least I think he does. Bree thinks he does.

My thoughts are swirling over and over in a never-ending whirlpool, so much so that I start to feel nauseated.

Bree grabs my hand and pulls me toward the bed, effectively snapping me out of my spinning thoughts. She sits next to me on the bed and wraps her arm around my shoulders.

"Stop overthinking things, Liv," she commands. "Everything will turn out exactly the way it needs to be." She rocks me back and forth slightly, her nurturing instincts kicking in. Part of me wants to chuckle at how much she's babying her crazy friend she hasn't seen in five years, and the other part wants to snuggle in closer, grateful for her friendship and her stability.

We sit there for a few minutes before Bree finally breaks the silence.

"So..." she grins knowingly. "How was it?"

I laugh before burying my face in the pillow and raising my hand up in the air, giving her a thumbs up.

She giggles hysterically. "Atta boy, Luke!"

Luke

I kissed her.

I freaking kissed her! I want to pound my fists against my chest and drag her back to the nearest cave like a Neanderthal. It was *just* a kiss, but it was damn near perfect.

I hope she doesn't regret it. *Regret me.*

Now that I've tasted her, I can't lose her. No one will ever compare. No one ever has, and I didn't even know what I was missing before.

I kissed her.

CHAPTER TWENTY-TWO

LIV

The next morning I decide to face one of my greatest fears and visit Susan. It's the moment I've been dreading for eight months.

I'm getting ready in the only bathroom upstairs and feel a little guilty procrastinating in such a highly coveted area.

I hear a gentle knock as I finish touching up my eyeliner. I've kept the makeup to a minimum with neutral eye shadow, a touch of liner, mascara, and some chapstick. My hair is in loose waves, hanging just above my shoulders, and I'm wearing a cute maternity dress with tights and knee-high boots.

I swing the door open, an apology on my lips for hogging the bathroom, when I see a very handsome Luke with his hand raised as he's about to knock again. He's in dark jeans and a light gray t-shirt with a zip-up olive hoodie on top. His sweatshirt makes his eyes pop, bringing out their forest undertones. A soft smile graces his lips as his gaze slowly slides down my body, taking in my appearance.

"You clean up nicely, Liv. I forgot what you looked like without sweats or yoga pants," he teases.

I snort and playfully hit him in the shoulder. "Hey, it's not my fault those are the only things I fit into!" I argue, pretending to be offended. "Five more weeks, my friend. Five more weeks."

"Yeah, yeah. You look good, though, Liv. Seriously," Luke says, lightly grasping my chin and holding my stare until he sees me acknowledge his compliment. A light blush covers my cheeks before I nod slowly, silently accepting his praise.

"You ready to meet Mother Gothal?" he teases, releasing my chin and stepping toward the stairs.

I snort, again, and follow him downstairs. "Not really."

Luke grabs my scarf from the coat rack near the front door and wraps it around me a couple of times, leaning in and kissing my nose. "Good. 'Cause there's no time like the present." He opens the door and ushers me to his car.

We don't say much on the drive over to Susan's house. We don't mention the kiss, even though this is our first time alone since last night. I'm grateful he doesn't bring it up. I'm already sweating enough as it is. I say a silent prayer of thanks to the deodorant gods before wiping my sweaty palms on my dress for the tenth time.

I practice my slow breathing and silently repeat my speech over and over again in my head.

Hey Susan! Did ya miss me? Congratulations! Adam decided to give you one more present from beyond the grave. You're gonna be a Grandma!

I groan, inwardly.

Luke pulls into the driveway of Adam's childhood home, and I begin to feel lightheaded.

So much for those breathing techniques.

The house is gorgeous and exactly how I remembered it. It's a large two-story covered in a classic red brick with a three car garage. There's a well-manicured front lawn that

Susan pays a fortune to be landscaped properly every year; it's covered with fresh snow for the time being. An elegant waterfall surrounded by classic black pebbles is one of the main focal points leading to the large front door as well.

Luke squeezes my hand across the center console before bringing it to his lips and kissing the inside of my wrist lightly. Goosebumps break out across my skin. I wish those lips were on mine, helping me forget the foreboding feeling in my gut.

Not the time, Liv.

"It's going to be okay, Sweetheart. Do you want me to come inside with you?"

I clear my throat, unable to speak, before nodding hesitantly.

If I can't find words now, what am I going to do when Susan answers that damn door?

Luke smiles reassuringly before exiting the car and opening my door. He places his hand on my lower back and guides me up the steps of the front porch.

I feel like my mouth is full of cotton balls. Every possible scenario is running through my frazzled brain, and not a single one is positive.

I'm screwed.

Luke grabs the ornate gold knocker on the heavy oak door and bangs it twice. I rock back and forth on my heels anxiously, more nervous than I've ever been in my entire life.

What if she's pissed?

I mean, of course she'll be pissed. But what if she's *really* pissed? What if she throws something? This woman is known for her tantrums.

What if she yells, and her neighbors all see?

Don't be ridiculous, I silently berate myself. She wouldn't cause a scene like that. What would the neighbors think?

What if she cries? I almost snort at the ludicrous thought. This woman doesn't cry. She doesn't have a sentimental bone in her body.

I just can't enter the house. That's when all hell will potentially break loose, and she might actually kill me. As long as there are possible witnesses, aka nosey neighbors, then I shouldn't be murdered within the next two minutes.

I breathe easier. Okay, just no going inside the house. That sounds like a solid plan. I can do this. I can do this. I nod my head reassuringly. *Piece of cake.*

We continue to wait not-so-patiently on the front porch, both of us unsure how my little confession will be taken.

After a minute or so, Luke looks at me, raising his brow and silently asking, *"Where the hell is she?"*

I shrug, wondering if we should just leave and forget about my lapse in judgment concerning telling my mother-in-law about her unborn grandbaby. He raises his hand toward the knocker, effectively putting the kabosh on my moment of clarity. The large oak door swings open and my mouth hits the floor, my eyes bugging out of my head.

Susan is still in a bathrobe, her hair a disheveled mess, the remnants of yesterday's makeup covering her face. Her eyes are swollen as if she's been crying, and fuzzy slippers are covering her un-pedicured feet.

Never in my life have I seen this woman so unkempt.

Luke clears his throat as I feel Susan's eyes zero in on my swollen stomach.

I bite my lower lip nervously, butterflies assaulting my insides. Actually, these aren't cute little butterflies, they're vicious vampire bats attempting to claw their way out.

I'm so stunned by her untidy appearance that my well-rehearsed speech vanishes into thin air.

Luke's hand gently nudges me forward, reminding me of my purpose. I lick my lips anxiously, preparing to talk, when Susan interrupts me.

"Is it his?" she whispers so quietly I have to strain to hear her. Her eyes bounce between Luke and my unborn baby.

It takes me a minute to understand her meaning. I wrap my arms around my belly, protecting him from the woman in the entryway.

"Are you freaking kidding me?" I whisper, astonished.

I'm used to the misconception. Hell, I expect it under any other circumstance. But I'm absolutely shocked Susan would honestly question whether this baby is Adam's or not.

I feel my blood begin to boil as I let her words sink in further, the front porch remaining silent.

"Are you honestly questioning whether this baby is Adam's or not?" My voice, along with my anger, rises. "Are you freaking serious?" I yell.

So much for not causing a scene.

"Why the hell would I be on your front porch if it wasn't Adam's, you insane woman? I almost didn't come here because of how little we saw eye-to-eye on things, but I thought, *'Adam would want his mother to know about her grandbaby.'* So I sucked up the courage to come here and tell you that you're going to be a grandma, and what do you do? You accuse me of cheating on my dead husband!"

Luke grabs my hips and pulls me back against him protectively. Whether he's protecting me from Susan, or afraid I'm going to physically assault my mother-in-law, I'm not sure. Regardless, I lean into his embrace, my back to his front, and try to calm down and not have an aneurysm. He rubs my arms comfortingly, and I close my eyes, the anger slowly seeping out of me.

Now, I feel utterly defeated. I lean into Luke and let him hold me up. I want to break down and cry, but refuse to let Susan see a single tear fall.

I knew Susan always hated me, but I never thought she questioned the love I had for her son. I breathe in deeply through my nose, releasing it through my mouth as I open my eyes once more and take in my mother-in-law.

Tears silently slide down her cheeks as she stares at my round stomach. Luke is still standing behind me, wrapping his arms around me protectively and resting his hands on my abdomen.

I let the image soak in for her, refusing to break the silence. If she's going to assume I have feelings for Luke, then I'm not going to soften the blow for her.

After a minute or so, although it feels like hours under her scrutinizing gaze, Susan finally looks into my eyes, remorse evident in hers.

"I'm sorry," she apologizes. "It wasn't fair of me to question you like that. It's just..." she glares at Luke, "*he's* always been in love with you, always trying to steal you away from my sweet Adam." Susan clears her throat, the look of disdain melting from her features before staring at me sheepishly, her eyes still glazed with fresh tears waiting to fall. "But that wasn't fair of me to question you like that. To judge your character. I've never been very fair to you," she confesses.

I'm taken aback by her apology. I was convinced the prideful woman didn't even know what those words were. I had never heard her utter them in the near-decade that I've known her. Part of me wants to smack her for being so unfair with Luke, but I rein in my desire, deciding to focus on her apology instead.

I silently wait for her to continue, completely dumb-struck by the turn of events. This was *not* how I was expecting my morning to go.

She swallows thickly before continuing. "Would you like to go to lunch with me today?"

I turn to Luke, wondering if this is some kind of trick.

"I can meet you somewhere. Anywhere you'd like," she rushes. "It would be nice to catch up, and I'd love to hear more about my grandbaby." Susan looks as though she might crumble to the hard marble tile covering her foyer if I refuse her invitation.

I'm not sure why this lunch date is so important to her, but I can't find the words to decline her offer. Adam would've wanted us to get along, and if she's extending the proverbial olive branch, then I should accept it.

I nod once, still unable to form words. We agree to meet at noon at a cute little café a mile or so from her house before she hesitantly closes the door behind her, effectively dismissing us.

Luke and I make our way back toward the car in silence, both of us shocked by how our interaction with Susan went.

I take a seat on the cold leather and can't help the question as it slips past my lips. "What did she mean, you keep trying to steal me away?" I ask after Luke starts the engine. I don't know why her comment bothered me so much, but it did.

I keep my eyes forward, staring at the dashboard, anxiously waiting for his reply.

"It's nothing," he states, but I can hear the lie on his lips.

I shake my head slightly, knowing he's keeping the truth from me, or at least some part of it.

"Liv."

I refuse to look at him.

"Liv," he repeats, sternly. "Look at me."

I can't.

"Listen. You don't understand part of Adam's and my relationship. I loved him like a brother, and he was a good guy. A *great* guy. But he was also a bit of an ass when he wanted to be, and I wasn't afraid to call him on his shit." He rakes his fingers through his hair angrily. "He wasn't good enough for you. And I didn't want you to get hurt."

My eyes narrow at his cryptic explanation.

"I don't understand."

"Liv. I don't want to do this. Please don't make me. Just know that we all make mistakes, and that neither of us wanted you to get hurt."

I look at him, confused. "Don't make you do *what*?"

He refuses to make eye contact with me, staring at the winding road in front of us. I guess I could blame it on the fact he's driving and it wouldn't be safe, but somehow it feels like it's more than that.

"Luke. What aren't you telling me?"

He shakes his head, turning toward me and pleading with his eyes. "Liv. Just forget it, okay? It's in the past. Can't we just leave it there? I just want you to be happy. That's all I've ever wanted."

I can't decide whether to push him on this, or to let it go. Once things are said, they can't be taken back. What's the saying? *Curiosity killed the cat.*

I bite my lip nervously. "Can you tell me why she thinks you were trying to steal me away?" I ask hesitantly, hoping I can get some answers without opening Pandora's Box.

Luke releases a breath, his tense shoulders relaxing

slightly. Apparently, my question is steering him to safer territory.

"That, I can do." He smiles tenderly at me, grasping my hand and squeezing it softly. "Adam knew about my feelings for you. Hell, I'm pretty sure everyone knew about my feelings, except you. You might think they're recent, but they aren't. I never made a move, as you know, but it always made Adam a little antsy anytime we were together. And anytime Adam felt threatened by someone, Susan would immediately go all Mama Bear on their ass and tear apart anyone who even thought about hurting her innocent baby boy." He snorts the last part, sarcasm thick in his voice as he lets go of my hand and anxiously runs his fingers through his hair again.

Apparently, we're circling dangerous territory once more.

"Susan is a great woman who thought her son could do no wrong. And while he was a great guy the majority of the time, he was far from perfect." He reaches over and squeezes my hand again, bringing it to his lips and kissing me gently before releasing it and turning on the radio.

Abruptly, our conversation is over, and I'm left thinking about his cryptic insight.

I guess we'll see how lunch goes.

CHAPTER TWENTY-THREE

LIV

I decide to leave my comfort blanket, aka Luke, at home for my lunch date with Cruella. He was nice enough to let me borrow his car and enjoyed teasing me about having to move the steering wheel higher so my belly could fit behind it.

Bastard.

I finish parking and make my way into the cute little café called Peggy's. They serve delicious pancakes all day, and my stomach rumbles as I am daydreaming about the fluffy cakes covered in warm maple syrup.

Yup. I think I'll have those.

I open the door and immediately see Susan sitting at a quaint little table in the corner.

The restaurant is decorated in a simple French theme. Pictures of the Eiffel Tower hang from the walls, and simple white tablecloths cover the tables. Colorful flowers in crystal vases are used as centerpieces. It's classy and elegant, perfect for Susan's taste.

I take a seat across from her and open my menu. I'm not sure why I'm looking at it since I've already decided what I want to order, but it seems like a good barrier between me and the woman across the table.

Susan folds her menu gracefully and places her dainty hands on top. She's not the woman I saw earlier this morning who was falling apart, but she's also not the lady I remember who was always so put together she seemed like a fancy painting.

Her fingers don't look freshly manicured, and she's wearing less jewelry than normal, just a simple gold chain around her long, slender neck and her wedding band. Her hair is showing a little gray at the roots, and her makeup is kept to a minimum instead of the usual masterpiece she regularly paints on a daily basis.

I'm not sure how I feel about this *new* Susan. I knew how to handle the old one, and I decide this one makes me a little uncomfortable. I liked the predictability, even if I didn't like the woman herself.

My back is rim-rod straight as I continue to stare at my menu, afraid to put it down. The waitress drops off two glasses of orange juice before pulling out her pad and pen to take our order.

I lick my lips hesitantly, placing the menu on the table. "I'll have the short stack, please. Bacon on the side." The waitress nods her head and turns to Susan.

"I'll have the same. Thank you," she states politely.

My jaw hits the floor. Again. Apparently, this is going to happen a lot with the *new* Susan. I've never seen her order anything other than an egg white veggie omelet and coffee.

The waitress leaves, and silence encompasses our table.

I tap my foot anxiously against the tile floor.

This is awkward.

Susan clears her throat. "It's interesting not having Adam here, isn't it? He was always the mediator between you and I." She takes a sip of her tart juice. "I'm not sure I've ever had a one-on-one conversation with you," she confesses.

I snort. *Nope. Pretty sure we haven't.* And now that I'm sitting in this little café, I can remember why.

"I take full responsibility for that," she continues. "I guess I was always a little protective of my baby boy and wasn't ready to give up being the only woman in his life at such a young age."

I remain silent, having nothing to contribute to the current topic. We *did* get married young. I won't deny that. We were nineteen. Practically babies. But we were in love. He proposed, and I couldn't say no.

"I apologize for that. I hope you understand that it was nothing personal. No one would have ever been good enough for Adam in my eyes. He was my entire world. I'm sure you'll understand that someday soon," she says, glancing toward my stomach.

I stay quiet.

"Is it a girl, or a boy? Do you know?" she asks, kindly. I can tell she's a little nervous to bring up the baby.

"It's a little boy." I smile shyly. Little Man has a habit of bringing a smile to my face every time I think about him.

She sighs, happily. "I'm glad. You would've made beautiful girls, too. But I'm excited that Adam left a little piece of himself with you. He was quite the handful as a child." She smiles wistfully, remembering a tiny Adam running around.

I laugh at her comment. "I can only imagine."

He was a handful as an adult.

"When are you due?"

"January 27th," I say, grinning. I'm not sure I've ever smiled this much in Susan's presence. Apparently, Little Man is taking on his father's role of mediator.

"That's wonderful." She grabs my hand delicately from across the table. It's kind of awkward, but I appreciate her effort. "I know I don't deserve this, considering how awful I was to you for all those years, but I would love to be part of this baby's life. If you'd let me." Her eyes are glassy as she stares at me earnestly.

I give her a non-committal shrug, still hesitant to trust someone who was so horrible for so many years.

"We'll see," I reply, squeezing her hand lightly, trying to soften the blow.

She nods slightly, trying to hide her disappointment. "I understand. I would be hesitant to trust me, too." She laughs sarcastically before releasing my hand.

"So where are you living? You disappeared after...." A tear slides down her face before she grabs her cloth napkin and dabs at it quickly.

"I'm actually roommates with Luke right now. We reconnected after the funeral and he offered me a place to stay." I'm unsure if mentioning Luke will bring back the *Mama Bear* or not.

"Of course he did," she replies haughtily. *Yup, Mama Bear's back.*

I find myself chuckling at her reply, secretly grateful Susan hasn't lost her spark. She was starting to scare me with her humility and meekness. It almost feels *good* to see a glimpse of the old Susan. The one with a backbone, even if it's at Luke's expense.

The waitress appears with our meals, and we dig in. The pancakes seem to melt on my tongue, and I moan in appreciation.

There's nothing like a good pancake smothered in maple syrup and butter.

"You know, you could've come to me," she states, her

posture reminding me of the Queen of England. She dabs the corner of her mouth with the cloth napkin and takes another sip of her juice.

"Who are you, and what have you done with my mother-in-law?" I tease. "You do remember who I am, right?"

She rolls her eyes (she never rolls her eyes) before relaxing into her chair and replying. "Well, maybe you couldn't have come to me *right* after the funeral. But if you had given me a few days, I would've come around. I was a mess afterwards. I felt like my whole world was falling apart. And I realized how alone I felt. None of the parties, none of the charities...none of it mattered. And the only family I had left, *you*, I had scared away. I wanted to reach out to you, but I was too ashamed of how badly I had treated you beforehand. I couldn't blame you for running away."

Her confession leaves me speechless. Again.

That seems to happen a lot around the *new* Susan.

"If I had known about the baby, how helpless you were, I would have swallowed my pride much sooner and offered to help. To do anything in my power to make sure you and your baby were taken care of. That's why I asked to meet you here." Susan looks at me contritely. "I want to offer my help. Anything you need. Support. Money. Someone to babysit. Anything." She grabs my hands, again, around the syrup and bacon, but this time it feels a little less awkward than the last.

"I'll have to let you know," I respond, squeezing her hands in return.

CHAPTER TWENTY-FOUR

LIV

I pull my phone out of my purse and check for any messages while I walk to Luke's car. I know Luke was a little worried about me meeting the Wicked Witch of the West by myself. Little does he know that it wasn't half as bad as I was expecting. She was actually quite *pleasant*.

Luke: *Hey Sanka, ya dead?*

I laugh at his *Cool Runnings* reference.

Liv: *Yeah, mon.*

Luke: *Ha ha. I'm glad you survived. How was it?*

I lean against Luke's car and contemplate my answer.

Liv: *Good? I think?*

Liv: *It was very enlightening.*

Liv: *She apologized for being an awful person.*

Liv: *She would love to help with Little Man in any way she can.*

I see the little bubble with dots and wait for his reply. Opening the car door, I throw my purse into the passenger seat before sliding into the driver's side. I immediately start the car and turn the heater on full blast, wiggling my bottom in hopes of making the seat-heater work faster.

My phone buzzes again.

Luke: Good! As long as you trust her, then I think that's great.

Luke: Just make sure you're careful.

Liv: I will, Mr. Bossy Pants! Don't worry!

Luke: I always worry about you.

Luke: BTW- Bree is driving me nuts! She keeps giving me mischievous looks and even gave me a chapstick. Did you tell her about last night?

Luke: Were my lips chapped?

I close my eyes as I relive last night, giggling lightly and sighing dreamily.

Liv: Maybe....

Luke: Maybe my lips were chapped? Or maybe you told her?

Luke: I don't want to be your dirty little secret.

Luke: But I'm cool getting dirty every once in a while. ;)

I laugh out loud at his ridiculous text.

Liv: Ha ha. Whatever, weirdo. Your lips weren't chapped.

Liv: They were delicious.

Liv: Now stop texting me! I need to drive home!

Luke: Friends don't let friends text and drive.

Luke: Buckle up!

Luke: And be safe!

Luke: But drive fast 'cause I may or may not strangle Bree before you get here.

Luke: Ps- She says Hi.

Luke: Okay, now I'm done.

Luke: See you soon!

Liv: You're not my dirty little secret. See you soon!

I roll my eyes before tossing my phone into my purse and backing out of the parking lot, a grin pasted on my face the entire ride home.

I get to the house just in time to see Bree throw a snowball at Luke's head, and a partially built snowman is under the tree where Luke and I kissed last night. I burst out laughing as he takes off after her and tackles her into the snow. I'm not sure what they're doing outside, but I'm suddenly very glad I ran that nearly red light a few minutes ago, or I would've missed the epic snow fight.

Stepping out of the car, I hear Breezy scream bloody murder and see Jake with his iPhone in the doorway, recording the whole thing. Sharon and Jim are laughing hysterically behind him, watching the chaos ensue.

This family is crazy. And I love every minute of it.

I'm sad when I think about going back with Luke in just a few short days. I love Luke's condo, but I'll miss his awesome family. They've kind of adopted me, and I kind of love them for it.

"What in the world are you guys doing?" I yell across the yard.

Luke is straddling Bree and shoving snow in her coat as she kicks and screams wildly. He looks over his shoulder at me and grins like the Cheshire cat.

"Bree kept asking me if I wanted to build a snowman. You know, like in *Frozen*? Anyway, I got so sick of her singing I finally dragged her outside to actually build one. And guess what the little brat does? She throws a snowball at me!" he yells, pretending to be annoyed.

Luke turns back toward his sister. "Jokes on you, little girl, 'cause I never lose a snowball fight." He throws his head back, laughing maniacally, making her admit defeat, then jumps up and runs toward me.

I laugh at his childlike playfulness, loving how carefree he is with his family.

He picks me up in a whirlwind and spins me around enthusiastically. I squeal with delight, shocked he can still lift me with a 20-pound basketball in the way. My arms are wrapped around his broad shoulders and I tuck my face into his neck as he gently sets me down. He leans forward so I can nuzzle him further. I breathe in his fresh scent, his cool skin tickling my nose. They must've been outside for a while.

"Hey you," he whispers into my hair.

I pull back slightly and stare at his piercing green eyes, a shy smile touching my lips.

"Hi."

He tucks a piece of my wavy hair behind my ear before placing a light kiss on my lips, his arms still holding me close.

I gasp at his familiarity, surprised he just kissed me in front of his family.

Even if it *was* just a peck.

"I've been wanting to do that for years, and since you gave me permission last night, I'm going to take full advantage of every opportunity from now on." He smirks, devilishly.

My shy smile turns into a full-on grin, and I shake my head back and forth.

"Well then, you better get to work."

I should've known better than to throw down the gauntlet like that. Especially to a man like Luke. I'm definitely not going to say I regret it though, because he immediately tangles his fingers in my hair with one hand, grabs my lower back with the other, and kisses me as if the world is ending. Hell, even if the world *was* ending, I would have no idea because every inch of my skin is already on fire from the heat of this kiss. His tongue tangles with mine, tasting every inch of me. I'm grateful for his firm grip, because I'm pretty sure I'd be a puddle on the pavement if he weren't holding me so tightly.

It's mind blowing. Incredible. All encompassing. Unforgettable. I would think of more adjectives, but I'm too busy experiencing the best kiss of my entire life.

He pulls back, a cocky grin on his face as I try to catch my breath.

"Whoa." I swallow thickly.

Talk about knocking a girl's socks off.

Or panties.

He chuckles before leaning in slowly and placing one more kiss on my lips. This one is sweeter. Softer. Less aggressive. More Luke. He lightly nibbles my lower lip before I feel his smile against my own.

Luke pulls back with the sweetest look on his face. Like he worships the ground I walk on. Like he adores me. Cherishes me. Maybe even *loves* me.

I hear hooting from the front porch, and I am quickly brought back to reality.

Did I really just make out with my not-boyfriend in front of his entire family?

I peek over Luke's shoulder and see Breezy proudly giving me the thumbs up and making kissy noises, while her parents cover Jake's eyes and laugh hysterically.

My cheeks immediately burst into flames.

Yup. I definitely did.

CHAPTER TWENTY-FIVE

LIV

After our little impromptu make-out session, I decide to take a nap in Bree's room. I'm exhausted from my eventful day and need a solid hour to recuperate. Or three.

Once I wake up, I look at the clock and see I'm late for dinner.

I rush to the bathroom, run a comb through my hair, and stumble down the stairs toward the dining room.

We eat a delicious traditional dinner with turkey and all the fixings. It is amazing, and I'm officially stuffed.

No one mentions the make-out session, thankfully. I'm able to pretend nothing is out of the ordinary, except for Luke's hand when he casually brushes it against my thigh underneath the table every few minutes.

I catch myself sighing every time he does it, which seems to spur him on. Before long, his hand is gently resting on my thigh. His thumb lightly rubbing back and forth rhythmically across my yoga pants.

Yes, I changed back into yoga pants. So sue me.

I keep wondering if we're just playing an epic game of

chicken, but then I catch glimpses of Breezy smiling wistfully in our direction, and I am reminded that these feelings are real and definitely not one-sided.

The only question I have now is, *Are we moving too fast?*

I still have so much to think about, and so many things to consider. I can't help but feel a little overwhelmed. Until I look at Luke. He must see all my emotions written across my face, because he gives my thigh a slight squeeze and smiles at me reassuringly, silencing all my chaotic thoughts.

"Want to go for a little drive? Or maybe watch a movie? I would ask you to go on a walk with me, but *someone* complained it was a little chilly last night." He nudges my shoulder playfully.

I laugh at his teasing before grabbing his hand and pulling him toward the couch. Christmas is tomorrow and I'm in the mood for another cheesy holiday movie.

Luke sits first, and I plop down next to him, throwing my legs into his lap and snuggling into the upholstery. He throws a fluffy blanket over us then grabs the controller and selects the Hallmark Channel. A grin tugs my lips as Luke rubs my feet and coos at Little Man.

The Liv Whisperer strikes again.

--

I wake up to find Luke snuggled behind me on the couch. By some miracle we both seem to fit while spooning.

The room is dark except for the twinkling Christmas lights hanging on the tree. I'd say it was "magical" if that wasn't such a cheesy description. *Eh, we did just watch a Hallmark Movie, so...yup.* The twinkling lights are definitely casting a magical glow around the empty room.

I smile at my wittiness, knowing no one would appreciate my lame humor except Luke, and maybe Bree.

I peek at the glowing display on the blu-ray player

informing me that it's well past midnight, and officially Christmas. I turn onto my back, causing Luke to stir before placing a gentle kiss on his lips and whispering, "Merry Christmas."

His sleepy green eyes flutter open before he smiles warmly, our faces mere inches away from each other. "Merry Christmas, Liv. I'm not gonna lie, I think I could get used to waking up with your lips on mine." He leans in and gives me a peck before lightly scrubbing his scruff against my cheek, teasingly.

I giggle at his affection and lift my hand, scratching his face like a puppy. "Well aren't you just the sweetest thing I've ever met? Yes you are! Yes you are!" I coo, using the same voice I usually reserve for cute little babies and cuddly animals.

He pretends to pant with his tongue out before licking my chin, causing me to push his face away and laugh even louder at his playfulness.

Luke has always been friendly and playful; but it feels like since our first kiss, a weight has been lifted from his shoulders. It's almost like he was holding himself back before. He's more carefree and open with his feelings now. I feel like, even though I've known Luke for forever, I'm getting a glimpse of a different side of him.

It's only making me fall for him more.

Before I can focus on my heart any longer, a Braxton Hicks contraction hits me like a freight train. I immediately curl into my belly and squeeze my eyes shut, attempting to breathe evenly as I wait for it to pass. It feels like a boa constrictor is tightening its grip across my midsection.

I open my eyes to see Luke's concerned gaze. "You okay, Sweetheart?"

I breathe deeply as the pain subsides and nod,

expressing that I am, indeed, okay.

Whoever said Braxton Hicks don't hurt is full of shit. I can only imagine what real labor will feel like.

Yikes.

"Let's get you up to bed, Liv. I'm sure Little Man isn't too happy about hanging off the couch half the night," he smirks while helping me sit up and pulling me to my feet.

Have I mentioned how I feel like a beached whale half the time?

"Thanks."

He shrugs off my gratitude, leading me up the stairs toward Bree's bedroom.

Once we reach the top, Luke places his hands on my stomach before giving me a stern warning. "If you keep having those contractions, you better tell me. I want to make sure we track how often and how painful they are. Dr. Fellows gave me strict orders." I can't help but grin at his bossy attitude.

Luke is a pretty laid back guy until you bring me, or my unborn baby, into the mix. That's when he goes a little crazy. I swear, I've even seen his fist twitch a time or two as if he's about to pound on his chest and claim us as his own. I kind of like how protective he is, though. It makes me feel this weird pinching sensation in my chest and behind my eyes.

I grasp his hands that are resting on my stomach and intertwine our fingers before resting my head on his broad chest. I breathe in deeply, taking in his masculine scent and rubbing my cheek against the soft cotton of his t-shirt.

"I will definitely keep you informed," I tell his delicious pecs. I nuzzle in closer before whispering more seriously, "And thank you, Luke. Thank you for taking care of me. Of us."

He releases my hands before bringing his palms up to

cradle my face. "I will always take care of you, Liv. Both of you. No matter what." He kisses me sweetly, his lips tenderly touching mine. I find myself holding my breath as he lowers his hands to my stomach and whispers, "Night, Little Man." His green eyes pierce my own as he looks at me. "Night, Liv."

He turns, slowly making his way into his room, and closes his door gently behind him. I continue to stare in his direction, whispering softly, "Night."

Luke

I had to walk away before I escorted her to my own room instead of Bree's.

I've had so many conflicting emotions swirling inside of me since this morning when we went to Adam's childhood home. I haven't been there in forever, but I couldn't believe all of the memories that hit me like a ton of bricks as soon as I pulled into his driveway.

And then for Susan to have the audacity to accuse me of trying to steal Liv? Painting me as the bad guy, instead of acknowledging what really went down?

I shake my head angrily.

It didn't help that Liv asked me about it in the car afterwards. I couldn't decide whether to come clean and feel a giant weight lifted from my shoulders, or to keep her in the dark, where she's safe and happily unaware of a mistake made so long ago that it shouldn't even matter anymore.

But if she thinks I lied to her? If I lose her for a mistake that wasn't even mine?

I swallow thickly and decide to stick my head in the sand.

No.

Not possible.

CHAPTER TWENTY-SIX

LIV

I wake up to very child-like Bree bouncing on the bed in pink polka dot pajamas and yelling, "Merry Christmas, ya filthy animal!"

I bury my head under my pillow and pull the covers up as far as they'll go, hoping Breezy will go away if I just ignore her.

Apparently, my wishful thinking is useless because she grabs the sheets and yanks them off the bed, leaving me a disheveled mess in an oversized t-shirt and sleep shorts.

"Rise and shine, Sunshine! It's Christmas, and we don't get to open presents unless everyone is in attendance! I don't care if you're pregnant or not, I want to start unwrapping!" she teases playfully, throwing me a fluffy pink bathrobe that also happens to be covered in polka dots.

I groan before lifting my arm high into the air from my lying position on the bed, silently requesting help sitting up. Bree laughs at my pathetic state before helping to pull me up.

"Chop, chop Livvy Lou! The day's a wastin'!" she yells over her shoulder before closing the door behind her.

I take a deep breath before chuckling to myself and shaking my head at my insane friend. Luke's sister is a total nut job, and I love her like crazy for it.

--

Christmas morning is awesome. It's fun to see all of Luke's family traditions, including everyone opening presents one at a time. It takes almost two hours to finish opening everything, and it's not because there are a billion presents. It's mainly because we spend so much time talking between each gift and enjoying one another's company that we forget to open another present until someone reminds us. And when I say *someone*, I mean Bree.

It's different than my Christmases with Adam and his mom. Everything was so forced, so structured, that it was hard to relax. Hell, I didn't even feel comfortable enough to take off my high-heeled shoes in her house. And here I am, drinking hot cocoa in a hot pink bathrobe and my hair, which still hasn't been brushed, in a small messy bun.

Don't get me wrong. Adam wasn't uptight like that at all. He was all about sweatpants and lazy Sunday mornings. He never cared if I followed the latest fashion trends, or if my nails were freshly painted.

I was the one who wanted to impress Susan, and when I finally gave up on that, I still put forth the effort to make Adam's life a little easier. I know it was hard to play referee between Susan and me every time we got together.

I take a sip of my hot chocolate before reminding myself how pleasant Susan was at breakfast. She asked if I could stop by sometime this afternoon so she could give me a few presents for the baby.

She promised it would be low-key, and that I didn't have to stay long if I didn't want to. She even mentioned that I could bring Luke if I *needed* to.

She said *needed* as though Luke has me on a tight leash or something, which you would know is ridiculous if you spent more than five minutes in the same room with him. I invited him anyway, just to ruffle her feathers. We might be on relatively good terms right now, but it's hard to remember that when I spent so long trying to get a rise out of her. Besides, I didn't invite him *just* to rile up Susan. I want him to be with me because when we're not together, I feel like a piece of me is missing. And when you lose someone you care about, you make more of an effort to be with the ones you love while you still can.

Luke grudgingly agreed to come with me, even though he was pretty hesitant to spend more time with Susan. I can't blame him. Those two definitely have some bad history. I'm not sure what the deal is, but I can't help feeling out of the loop with all their cryptic comments.

I shrug it off before heading upstairs to shower. I might refuse to wear high heels in her house now, but I should still look somewhat presentable. Smelling like a hobo might be pushing my luck.

Unfortunately, pants are a no-go for me. I can't stand the maternity elastic waists, but I do have a cute gray and white maternity dress that grazes the floor. I pair it with black flats and a black puffy jacket, my hair in its signature loose curls.

I apply some chapstick and mascara before heading down the stairs toward Luke and his family. I can hear his husky laughter as I make my way down the hall to the family room.

Sneaking a gingerbread cookie, I lean against the door-frame and watch Luke interact with his family. They're just finishing up a board game with tiny trains, and I smile as I take in how handsome he is. The light from the window is caressing his skin, giving him a warm glow and highlighting his chiseled features.

He and Bree are arguing over who got the longest route in the game as Jake counts the trains, announcing himself the victor before Luke teases him playfully about cheating.

It takes a minute before anyone notices me, but I don't mind being an observer in this moment. I take my time nibbling on my cookie and enjoy the happiness that radiates from the room.

I hope I can create a fraction of this much joy in my home with Little Man. It'll definitely be quieter, since it will just be the two of us, but I want my baby boy to have happy childhood memories like Luke does with his family. I hope he never has to experience the loneliness that was my constant companion while growing up.

I catch Luke staring at me from across the room, right after finishing my last bite of gingerbread. He makes his way over to me, purposely bumping the board and causing the tiny trains to scatter, effectively ending all arguing about who won. Luke wraps me in a hug, holding me closely as his siblings curse at him from across the room.

I smile softly and peek up at him, seeing a mischievous grin on his face. He's obviously pleased with his not-so-subtle maneuver. Luke leans forward and kisses me softly, slowly nibbling the corner of my mouth before pulling away and licking his lips.

"You taste like cookies," he grins, affectionately.

I nod, embarrassed at being caught eating more sweets. *I swear this baby is addicted to sugar already!*

"Let's grab a few more before we hit the road," he states, bouncing his eyebrows up and down. He grabs my hand and pulls me into the kitchen where the countertops are covered with a variety of treats.

Luke grabs a half-dozen cookies before nudging me out the front door and to his car outside.

--

I may or may not have finished the last cookie as we pull into Susan's driveway.

Luke smirks knowingly, well aware of my closet sugar addiction, and pulls me into another steamy kiss across the center console. He doesn't release me until I'm breathless, his grin still firmly in place.

"Tease," I accuse, frustrated.

Damn these pregnancy hormones!

His smile widens before he shrugs nonchalantly. "Is it my fault that if I want to eat a cookie, I have to steal the taste from your tongue?"

I bite my lip, my cheeks reddening as he bursts into laughter, proud of himself for embarrassing me with his boldness.

I turn away from Luke, grabbing the door handle in hopes of escaping the car. He leans over the console, his entire torso on the passenger side, and pulls me toward him once more, effectively preventing my escape.

He grabs my chin with authority, both forceful and gentle at the same time, like I'm precious, but he refuses to let me go until he's ready to do so. "I already told you that I would take every single opportunity to kiss you now that you've given me permission. This includes using the excuse to taste the sweet spice still lingering on your lips from your adorable sugar habit."

He gently presses his lips to mine, his calloused hands cradling my face. He pulls away slightly, though I can still feel his breath against my cheeks. "I'm pretty sure you could eat onions and garlic every day for the rest of your life, and you'd still be the sweetest thing I've ever tasted," he whispers huskily, his gorgeous green eyes pinning me in my passenger seat.

The tension is so thick in the small sedan, you could cut it with a knife. Luke swallows thickly, obviously as affected by our close proximity as I am. He kisses my forehead, his lips lingering before releasing me, his head brushing against the roof of the car as he sits back in his own seat.

Luke opens his door and makes his way around the car as I try to catch my breath.

The only thought running through my head is, *Your taste is pretty addicting, too.*

Luke opens my door and ushers me to the front porch as I experience a weird déjà vu feeling from having done this the day before.

However, this time Susan answers the door almost immediately as if she has been hovering in her entryway, not-so-patiently waiting for our arrival.

She's wearing a fancy plum-colored dress with a sweetheart neckline that reaches just above her knees and a matching gold bracelet and necklace. Her ensemble reminds me of the *old* Susan, until my gaze reaches her feet, which are refreshingly bare. A small smile touches my lips as the *new* Susan immediately pulls me into an embrace.

My arms hang awkwardly at my sides, unsure how to react in such a foreign position. I turn my face to look at Luke, his shocked expression mirroring my own. I'm pretty sure she's only hugged me one other time in my entire life, and it was more for show than an honest expression of love or affection.

The hug was at Adam's and my wedding. The photographer had insisted on an intimate moment between mother and daughter-in-law, Susan welcoming me into the family with open arms. Adam had framed it for Susan after we received the pictures, laughing at our awkward posture.

I can't help but chuckle at how he would perceive our current embrace as well. I hesitantly return the hug, patting her back cautiously. My eyes are still glued to Luke's as he covers up his snickering with a fake cough.

Susan releases me, smiling widely as she sweeps her arms wide open, welcoming us into her home.

"Come in, come in. I wouldn't want you to catch a cold. That couldn't be good for the baby!" she fusses, ushering us inside the foyer.

The house looks exactly how I remember it. Olive green walls, gold fixtures, and textured marble tile covering the floors. The only difference is a chunky gold picture frame that's been added to the hand-carved mahogany entry table at the base of the stairs.

I take a step closer and examine the image. It's a picture of Adam and me at our wedding, shoving cake into each other's faces. We're both smiling from ear to ear, laughing hysterically at the mess we'd made. The photographer captured the moment perfectly.

I'm stunned as I consider Susan's photograph choice. She hated that picture. She had warned me before the festivities not to make a fool out of myself, and her precious son. How I would always regret getting frosting on my perfectly white wedding dress if I didn't act like an adult and eat the dessert gracefully.

I can't help but roll my eyes as I remember how proper the woman was...*is*. How she whispered that her son was marrying a child, how she didn't approve of the marriage, and how she had assumed we'd be divorced in a fortnight.

A fortnight.

Her words, not mine.

As I continue to stare at the picture, I hear Susan's bare feet pad across the tile until she's standing next to me.

"You made him happier than I could have ever dreamed. I'm sorry I didn't see it at the time," she confesses quietly, examining the photograph. "All I ever wanted was for him to be happy, but I was too stubborn to admit that all he ever needed was you."

I swallow thickly before placing the gaudy frame back on the entry table. I peer over my shoulder as Luke stands by the door with his hands in his pockets. I hold out my hand, motioning him to come closer. He immediately complies, intertwining his fingers with my own.

I look back at Susan, her eyes staring at our interlaced hands before clearing her throat and walking toward the living room.

Luke squeezes my hand before following. The room is extravagantly decorated with a large fake Christmas tree in the corner. I assume it isn't real, anyway. Susan would never have allowed pine needles to ruin her plush cream carpet.

I shake my head slightly, attempting to stop myself from assuming the worst of her. She's been nothing but kind to me lately, and I need to return the favor.

"Come sit down. Make yourselves at home." Susan gestures to the fancy coffee-colored leather couches.

Luke and I sit hesitantly, my hand tightly gripping his. He squeezes it once before letting go and resting his arm on the back of the couch behind me, gently running his fingers across my shoulders. His soothing touch instantly relaxes me, causing me to melt into the leather cushions and, more importantly, into Luke's side.

Susan takes a deep breath, obviously trying to hide her frustration as she looks at Luke and I snuggling on her couch. I don't want to make her uncomfortable, but I also don't want to lose Luke's touch. He grounds me. Makes me feel like I can tackle anything. Makes me feel *whole*.

"Thank you for inviting us," I say politely, trying to break the tension.

She nods curtly before attempting to smile, as poised as ever. "Of course. How could I not? I've been dying to spoil my only grandbaby," she gushes, sweetly.

I look over at the Christmas tree in the corner, just now noticing the piles and piles of presents hidden underneath.

"Are those *all* for my Little Man?" I shriek, blown away by the sheer number of gifts.

She nods enthusiastically. "Of course, they are!"

I turn and look at Luke, feeling like a fish out of water.

I can't accept these. There are too many. They're too huge.

"How do you expect me to get them home?" I ask, feeling overwhelmed by the sheer number of gifts.

"What do you mean, home?" she questions. "I thought you *were* home." Her gaze bounces between Luke and me.

I lick my lips, my brows furrowed. "I live with Luke," I state, although it seems to come out as a question.

He squeezes my shoulder reassuringly. "Yeah, she's coming home with me. We leave tomorrow, actually." He sounds so casual, but I can feel the way his muscles tense under his grey button-up shirt.

Susan waves her hand, quickly dismissing Luke's comment. "That's nonsense, Liv. You said so yourself. You only went to live with Luke because you had no other options. Obviously, that isn't the case anymore. I still have Adam's inheritance, and he would never forgive me if you didn't have access to it, for the child's sake. It was actually your main gift. I had the bank put your name on the account. You can get a place of your own tomorrow if you want. Something closer to home. Something closer to *family*." It's obvious she's referring to herself.

My eyes bounce between my mother-in-law and Luke. I don't know why this new information has brought me to question where I'll be living, but it does. Luke only invited me to live with him because he felt obligated. Because he felt like he needed to clean up Adam's mess.

But that was before we *kissed*.

Maybe he feels differently now?

It's not like we've had '*the talk*' or anything. I don't even really know where we stand. And I'm not sure where I *want* us to stand.

I feel like I'm walking on a tightrope of emotions, and I could plunge either way at any moment.

On one hand, I want to feel independent. I want to do something on my own without the need to rely on someone. I don't want to be a burden to anyone, let alone my best friend. I don't want to hold Luke back, or make him feel obligated to step into the 'father' role. He didn't sign up for that. And I don't want him to ever regret helping me when I needed him most, from a financial standpoint as well as an emotional one.

But on the other hand, I don't want to lose the only person I really care about. Luke means everything to me. He was a huge part of my world back then, and he's become an even larger part since we've reconnected.

As soon as these thoughts enter my head, guilt quickly follows. I start to question if I'm replacing Adam with his best friend. And I still remember what Luke said the moment before we kissed for the first time, that he was okay with being second place.

I don't want Luke to feel that way. It isn't fair to him, and it definitely isn't true. There isn't a first or second place.

There are just two separate men that I've loved, and will continue to love for the rest of my life. They've always held different pieces of my heart.

Holy shit. Did I just use the L-word?

I think I've always known that I've loved Luke a little bit, but to come to that realization while sitting on my dead husband's mother's couch is a bit too much to handle.

I feel so confused.

And dizzy. I feel dizzy.

Like I'm on a Tilt-a-Whirl and might vomit all over said plush cream carpet if I don't clear my head soon.

Before I can get a grip on my overwhelming emotions, Susan's crisp voice interrupts my swirling thoughts.

"Liv, honey. I think you and I should talk in private," she states cautiously, as though talking to a skittish animal.

"No chance in hell will I let you do that," Luke growls protectively, his arm wrapping around my shoulders.

"Why not? Afraid I'll turn her against you for good? Show her your true colors?" Susan spits, angrily. "How you would lie? Cheat? Steal? Do whatever was in your power to take her away?"

Mama Bear is back with a vengeance.

I'm shocked by how drastically her tone changed from carefully handling me like a china doll, to practically attacking Luke as if he were a cockroach under her shoe.

I want to ask what she's talking about, but I'm frozen to the spot. My mind is attempting to comprehend her cryptic statement while still grappling to get a handle on my fraying emotions.

"Don't listen to her, Liv. She's trying to manipulate you. I think we should leave," he whispers calmly into my ear while attempting to comfort me.

"Don't listen to me?" Susan sneers, obviously overhearing Luke. "You think he's a shining knight with a white horse coming to rescue you? He's a wolf in sheep's clothing, Liv. He even made up some ridiculous story about Adam cheating on you before graduation. Can you believe that?" she scoffs, oblivious to the bomb she just dropped out of nowhere.

Her statement shocks my system enough to push me to stand, slipping Luke's arm from my shoulder, my mind reeling. I turn and look at Luke, silently demanding an explanation. He looks up at me with glassy green eyes, silently pleading with me. "Liv. Don't make me do this."

I swallow thickly. "Do what, Luke?" I whisper, holding his gaze.

"Don't make me break your heart for him."

I shake my head in denial. Not wanting to hear his explanation, but needing the truth more.

"Tell me what you mean," I demand, surprised by my steely voice.

Luke runs his fingers through his thick hair, pulling slightly on the ends before speaking.

"The night your grandma died, remember I found you in the girl's bathroom and you told me you never wanted to be alone?"

I nod, listening.

"I knew you needed Adam, so I texted him, but he never replied. He was supposed to be home for a family dinner. I drove to his house. *This house*," Luke scoffs, taking in the great room. "I rushed in here without knocking, knowing you needed him to comfort you, and found him with someone else." He looks at the ground shamefully, almost as if Adam's transgression is his own.

I'm too shocked to speak. But I don't need to as Luke rushes on.

"I'm so sorry, Liv. I was pissed as hell that he would betray you like that, and we got into a fight. I told him that he didn't deserve you. That he let the best thing that ever happened to him slip through his fingers. I could see the guilt written all over his face. I know he had been drinking; the room reeked of alcohol. And you know Adam never drank. Not like that's any excuse, but...." His voice trails off, leaving me to fill in the blank.

Luke shakes his head, not wanting to relive the moment.

"Adam looked me in the eyes, and I could see how at war he was with himself. He felt guilty as hell, but was defensive too. You know how he never liked to be wrong, Liv. He said, *'You let her slip through your fingers first. You could've had her, but you were too much of a pussy to do anything about it.'* And he was right, Liv. Adam was right. I lost you before I ever even had you. But you seemed so happy with Adam, and I didn't want to ruin that." Luke stands up and starts pacing around the room like a caged beast, running his shaky hands through his hair.

"And he loved you. I know he did. You could see how much he regretted it. I told him about your grandmother, and I could see his heart breaking for you right before my eyes. He decided then and there that his little slip-up would be just that. A one-time slip-up. He wasn't going to break up with you right after your Grandma died. He didn't want to leave you alone. He was just feeling so much pressure from his mom," Luke glares at Susan, "and going away to college. He had never been with anyone but you. It's no excuse, but it practically tore him in two. He spent the rest of his life trying to make it up to you."

Luke looks as if his heart is breaking, right along with mine.

"He loved you, Liv. He did. He was just a stupid kid, who

did a really stupid thing, and regretted it for the rest of his life," Luke whispers, defeated.

I try to comprehend his confession, but one thing keeps coming back.

"So, you lied to me?" I ask, tears streaming down my cheeks.

"No, Liv. I mean, yes," he chokes out, "but, I didn't mean to. It just wasn't my secret to tell. I wanted to. But I knew you loved him. I didn't want to see your heart get broken, especially after everything else you were going through," he apologizes, silently begging me to forgive him.

I shake my head in denial. This can't be happening.

The only reason Adam and I stayed together was because he felt too guilty to break up with me?

We freaking got married. I'm having his effing baby. Did he ever even love me?

"Don't be ridiculous, Luke. Adam would never do that. See, Liv? See what I was talking about? See the insane lies Luke has been spinning? Making my precious Adam into the bad guy? He loved you! And I honestly don't remember pressuring him *that* much," Susan interrupts, as though she has any right to be involved in this conversation.

I had forgotten she was even in the room.

I quickly wipe the tears from my eyes, willing myself to become numb for the next few hours. Long enough to get alone and digest this new information by myself.

I feel betrayed.

But I believe him. He isn't lying.

Susan is just a proud mother who is unable to see the flaws in her only son.

I remember how things were a few weeks before graduation. I remember Adam becoming more distant. I remember

Susan pressuring him like hell to break up with me so he could sow his wild oats in college.

And I remember the pain I felt when my grandmother died. I remember Luke holding me, promising me that everything would be all right. That he would make it all better.

And I guess this was his way of keeping that promise.

But it also broke my heart in the process.

I feel like the last five, almost six, years have been a lie. A big. Giant. Lie.

Without a single word, I make my way to the guest bathroom to compose myself. I can hear Luke and Susan whisper-yelling at each other as I close the door gently behind me.

After using the restroom and splashing cold water on my face, I'm reminded of the morning of Adam's funeral. How I splashed cold water on my face that morning, too. How I gave myself a little pep talk, promising myself that I would figure things out. That I needed to get my shit together and get through the next few days because they were going to happen, whether I wanted them to or not.

I look at myself in the mirror, taking note of my red, swollen eyes. I run my fingers through my hair before pulling it into a ponytail. I breathe in and out slowly, deeply, and count to one hundred before smoothing down my maxi dress and opening the door.

Luke is waiting in the entryway with my black puffy jacket and his thick winter coat.

Susan is nowhere to be seen, although I think that's for the best until I can sort through the myriad of emotions fighting inside of me.

Luke holds up my jacket, allowing me to slip my arms through the sleeves. After it's completely on, he places his hand on my lower back and leads me to his car, which is already running. Apparently, he had come outside earlier to warm it up. I'm grateful for his thoughtfulness as I let the heat soak into my numb soul.

The car is silent except for the engine's low hum as we make our way back to his parents' house.

I'm sure he would kill to know what I'm thinking right now. But, honestly? I'm not really sure what I'm thinking. The only thing I'm choosing to focus on is my Little Man.

I rest my hand on my stomach and savor every little kick, every tiny nudge, refusing to let my tears fall.

CHAPTER TWENTY-SEVEN

LIV

When we finally reach Luke's childhood home, I still haven't uttered a word. I go inside, pack my bags, and request an Uber to come pick me up.

Thankfully, his family is nowhere to be seen. I think they're at Luke's grandparents' house. It is still Christmas, after all.

Merry freaking Christmas.

I make my way down the stairs, my luggage in hand. Luke hears me lumbering down the steps and walks down the hall from the kitchen, eyeing my suitcases in disbelief.

"Liv. Where're you going?" he murmurs, hesitantly. "Do you want to leave right now? I'll go pack my stuff. Give me ten minutes and we'll head home. My parents will understand. No big deal." He comes over and grabs my luggage from my hands, gently placing it by the front door.

I shake my head, refusing to let any tears fall.

Not yet.

You can break down in the car, but not yet.

I close my eyes, willing the tears to disappear when I feel Luke's strong hands cradle my face.

"Liv. Don't cry, Sweetheart. I've got you," he whispers, placing a gentle kiss on my forehead, reminding me of all the times he's caught me when he could have easily just let me fall.

I was never his to worry about. And yet, he still took on that responsibility.

A sob catches in my throat as I try to freeze this moment in time. Not the heartache that's eating me from the inside out, but the feel of his soft lips tenderly brushing my forehead.

I shake my face in his hands, trying to pull myself together. He rests his forehead against mine.

"What are you doing, Liv? Where are you going to go?"

I shrug my shoulders, feeling the weight on them. "Doesn't matter. Just...away. I think," I breathe shakily.

"You can't leave me, Liv. I need you. Don't you know that by now? I've always needed you. I can't let you go. I can't be without you again," he pleads, his vulnerability ripping my heart out.

I lick my lips slowly, trying to gain the courage to open my eyes and see his green ones staring back at me.

I take a deep breath before peeking at Luke, tears silently streaming down my cheeks.

"You lied to me." He closes his eyes in shame. "Adam lied to me." He slumps his shoulders, defeated.

"I don't know what to think. I don't know what to do. All I can focus on right now is my baby who will be here within a month." I try to swallow past the lump in my throat.

"Then let me drive you home, Liv. You need to be near Dr. Fellows."

"I can find a doctor here. It's not the first time someone's moved mid-pregnancy, and it won't be the last," I say, steeling my resolve.

"Please, Liv. Don't do this. I finally got you," he whispers, his hands still cradling my face.

The moment feels so intimate, and I know I need to pull away to protect my throbbing heart, but I can't bring myself to break free from his comforting touch. It's like a soothing balm to my aching soul.

Let me savor him for one more minute.

I take a deep breath, squeezing my eyes shut and trying to think clearly while still under the spell that Luke casts on me any time we're in the same room.

"I need to be on my own for a little while. I need to come to terms with the fact that my dead husband lied to me. That he cheated on me. That my entire marriage may or may not have been completely out of obligation. I look back on our wedding day and can't help but wonder if his happiness was genuine, or if he was just the greatest actor in the world. I need to accept that I may never truly find the answers I'm looking for. And most importantly, I need to find a way to forgive Adam for his gut-wrenching mistake. I can't raise Adam's son if I'm rotting from the inside out with guilt, shame, and hatred toward his father. Guilt because I'm so angry at him. I want to yell, kick, and scream at him, but he's not even here to defend himself, or to apologize. I feel shame because I now have to wonder, for the rest of my life, if my husband ever truly loved me. And hatred because he lied to me; he broke my heart and left me here alone to pick up the pieces. I have all these emotions fighting inside of me, and I don't think I can focus on the man I loved who shattered me and work toward forgiving him if I'm with another man who I think I might be in love with, too."

Luke gasps at my confession, but I continue on.

"And honestly, Luke? I'm mad at you, too. How could you keep this from me? How could you cover for him? I thought I meant more to you than that." I swallow thickly, Luke's warm hands catching my salty tears, his shoulders slumped in defeat as though my words physically assault him.

"I'm going to go now, Luke. I want to be with you more than anything else in the world, but I need to lay the past to rest if I ever want to be able to move forward and have a healthy relationship. And I need to figure out if I can forgive you, too."

I hear a honk, indicating my ride is here, and gently step out of Luke's grasp. I can't stand to say goodbye, so I simply hold his gaze, hoping to express, without words, how much I love him, how sorry I am, and how much I'm hurting.

I can see the pain in his eyes mirroring my own. I try to contain my sobs while I pick up my luggage and carry it to the black sedan waiting in the driveway.

The car pulls onto the street as I stare out the window, watching the man I love fade into the distance.

Luke

I angrily pace the hallway, arguing with myself over the right way to handle this situation.

Do I go after her?

Give her space?

Demand she come home where she belongs?

Tell her I love her and can't live without her?

Again.

I tried living without her before. It was hell. I can't go back to living that way. But I will, if that's what she thinks she needs. I would do anything for her.

Do I attempt to explain how much Adam really did love her? That he was stupid and made one childish mistake? It was inexcusable, but he was a stupid seventeen year old, and I *know* he regretted it.

That's what kills me the most. How can she honestly think no one could love her? Does she really think Adam would throw away his life to be with someone he didn't love? It wasn't like that. I *knew* Adam. I saw the way he looked at her. He loved her. He was an idiot, and he made a mistake. But he loved her.

If he didn't, he would've waited a few months before breaking it off. He wouldn't have asked her to marry him, voluntarily throwing his life away out of guilt for leaving a girl behind that he didn't really care about.

But then I question my sanity when I honestly consider defending him to her. She has every right to be angry. To hate him. To kick and scream. To curse his name.

But she's also right that her anger will affect her baby, and how he perceives his deceased father. That her hatred will slowly eat away at her, and will possibly affect her future relationships. Hopefully one with me...if she can ever forgive me.

She had a right to know.

But Adam didn't have the decency to tell her.

And neither did I.

I can't idly sit back and watch her go through this alone.

Hell, Little Man could arrive any day now. I can't leave her.

But I also need to respect her wishes.

Rock, meet hard place.

I run my fingers through my hair, cursing Susan for opening up this can of worms. But maybe it's good that Liv finally knows the secret I've been carrying for far too long.

She had a right to know. I just wish I wasn't the one who had to tell her, to break her heart.

It wasn't fair. And now I just have to hope it didn't ruin what we could have had.

We were so close.

Why does it feel like I've lost her for good?

CHAPTER TWENTY-EIGHT

LIV

The Uber driver dropped me off at a nearby hotel that didn't look too run-down. Thankfully, I have a little money saved up from my secretary job and can afford a few nights here before figuring out what I'm going to do.

My phone has been ringing off the hook. Between Luke, Bree, and Susan, I haven't had a moment of peace. I finally decide to turn off my phone after convincing Breezy not to dig up Adam's corpse and castrate him for me. While I appreciate the sentiment, I don't want her desecrating any graves. And let's be honest, I wouldn't put it past her.

I've also decided I'm going to take Susan up on her offer concerning Adam's inheritance. He might've been an asshole that never loved me, but I know he would've never shied away from his responsibility as a father. He would've insisted on taking care of us, which means I'm going to allow him to do it beyond the grave by providing financial support.

And honestly? He kind of owes me one.

The stressful day has definitely caught up to me. I'm

absolutely exhausted. I forego a shower and curl up into a ball on the queen-sized bed, breathing deeply through my Braxton Hicks. I read somewhere that stress can cause more contractions, and I can personally testify it's true.

Thanks a lot, guys.

I shove a pillow under my belly and let the tears roll down my cheeks silently, grateful for the black-out curtains that will hopefully allow me to sleep.

The next morning, I wake up with puffy eyes and feel dehydrated from all my crying the day before. I had a hard time sleeping, tossing and turning all night, finding it impossible to turn off my brain for five minutes so I could get some decent rest. I finally decide it's time to face the music as I stare at the alarm clock on the nightstand and turn on my phone.

I ignore every text from Luke, and there are a lot of them. I know he's worried about me, but I don't think I can handle his attention right now. And if I'm being honest, he's kind of on my shit list. Adam's betrayal has made me question each and every interaction I've had with both him and Luke. What was real? What was genuine? Anything? Everything? Nothing? How could he have kept this from me? I'm becoming overwhelmed again, and it's not even noon.

So, I decide to call Susan.

She picks up on the first ring, and we have a quick conversation where she asks long, exhausting questions, and I answer with single syllables. She apologizes profusely for being a B-word (I'm trying to cut back on my naughty language, thanks to my Little Man) and I decide to throw her a bone by grudgingly accepting her apology.

After her explanation, we figure out the money situation. Thankfully, she's very gracious and insists on dropping off the paperwork at the front desk of my hotel. I'm not ready to see her yet, and am frankly pretty pissed at her still. She might not have known the can of worms she was opening, but she still handed Luke the freaking opener, insisting he spill the beans.

I'm also not in the mood to look for an apartment, but now that I have a seven-pound ticking time bomb that will wait for no one, I need to figure out my living situation before this baby decides to make an appearance.

I was counting on Luke to set up the crib, help paint the nursery, research bottle options, and pick up diapers.

I'm a little ashamed at how much I relied on him, and how I kind of assumed I would still live with him after the baby is born.

He must've thought I was crazy. Why would he willingly step into the father role after Little Man was born? This baby isn't his. He knows this. I know this. How did I somehow space out on that not-so-minor detail? Not the fact that he isn't the father, but the assumption he'd want to help. How could I assume he'd want anything to do with a postpartum woman and a new baby? I must've lost my marbles.

I shrug off my morose thoughts, refusing to beat myself up. I can't change the past, but I can definitely learn from it.

I'm not going to assume he wants anything to do with me, or Little Man. I won't, even if it tears me up inside.

What I need to do is move on, by myself, and be the independent woman that I need to be. I'm going to be a single mother. I knew that in the beginning, but I somehow had forgotten, the longer I was around Luke.

To be fair, he did insist on coming to all of my appointments. He read every weekly update about how my baby was developing, receiving notifications on his fruit equivalent. He spent every night snuggled on the couch with me, whispering to Little Man, hoping to gain a connection with him. I never asked him to do any of that. That was all him.

And I love him for it, I begrudgingly admit to myself, feeling a scowl on my face.

I'm pulled from my thoughts after receiving another text, my phone vibrating in my hand.

Breezy: *Alright, girly. I can't allow you to wallow by yourself. It's against the girl code.*

I smile slowly before my phone vibrates again.

Breezy: *Where art thou? I'll bring chocolate.*

Breezy: *And pizza.*

Breezy: *And I won't tell Luke.*

Breezy: *We'll make him sweat a lil bit.*

I only hesitate for a minute before replying.

Liv: *Hotel on Main. Bring donuts too.*

Bree: *Gotcha covered Livvy Lou.*

Within an hour, someone is banging on my door. I walk over to it, peeking through the peephole before swinging the door open. Bree's hands are ridiculously full. She's balancing a cardboard pizza box in her hands, and two giant grocery sacks are hanging on her arm.

I laugh at her slightly disheveled appearance. She's wearing a bright red beanie and her cheeks are flushed from exertion. Her chocolate hair is in messy curls hanging down her back, and a large black winter coat swallows her whole. Black yoga pants and bright-red snow boots finish her ensemble.

I grab the pizza box from her hand as she shoves the door open the rest of the way with her hip and drops the grocery sacks on the queen-sized bed in the center of the room.

She flexes her muscles victoriously at me and proudly states, "I've still got it! Do you have any idea how hard that was to carry all your crap from my car, to the elevator, push the stupid button, walk down the never-ending hallway, and knock on your door with my foot? Let me tell you, it wasn't easy, but my Incredible Hulk muscles never let me down!" She flexes her skinny noodle-like arms once more, kissing her non-existent biceps before pushing me teasingly to the side and stepping into the hotel bathroom. "And now I have to pee," she smirks, closing the door in my face.

I chuckle at her crazy antics, grateful for her fun sense of humor. She reminds me of Joy from *Inside Out*, if she was inebriated the entire time.

I take a slice of pizza and moan as the cheese touches my tongue. It's absolutely delicious, and I am starving! I know I'm going to regret my food choices later today, thanks to acid reflux, but right now I couldn't care less.

I hear the toilet flush as I bite into my second slice. Bree bounces into the room and grabs her own before sitting next to me on the bed. She kicks her feet up and rests against the headboard before devouring her slice.

"So, Luke's a wreck," she states matter-of-factly, her mouth full.

I glare in her direction, placing my half-eaten slice in the box. Apparently, I've lost my appetite.

"Way to skip the small talk, Bree," I growl.

"We both know I'm not known for my subtlety," she replies cheekily, taking another bite of pizza and causing the cheese to string between her mouth and the slice.

I roll my eyes before picking at some pizza crumbs on my large hoodie and refusing to address the elephant in the room named Luke.

"Look." She bounces onto her knees, facing me fully and gaining all of my attention, her pizza still in hand.

"Luke was an ass. What he did is one hundred percent

wrong. He shouldn't have kept that from you, but he didn't feel like it was his place to tell you, especially when his feelings were mucking up everything," she says, her gaze trying to portray her honesty. "But you gotta cut him a little slack. The big idiot loves you, Liv. He's pissed at himself for hurting you."

I bite my lower lip, battling myself internally on how I should reply. "I know he does, and I know he's your brother, and you don't want to see him hurting. Hell, I don't want to see him hurting, either. That isn't my intention at all. I'm just not ready to let it go quite yet." I warily look at her, gaging her reaction.

She shrugs one shoulder, looking more serious than I've ever seen her. "I'm here for you, Liv. I love my brother, and I know you do, too. But if you're not ready to see him? I get that. I know we weren't super close in high school, but I'm here for you. And if you want to make him sweat, then I completely support you in that endeavor," she grins mischievously. "In fact, I have a brilliant idea."

I examine her cautiously, afraid of what this girl might consider a *brilliant idea*.

She grins wider under my scrutiny. "Here's the deal. Luke's not leaving without you. He loves you and is absolutely terrified you're not coming home. But he's also wasting all his vacation time waiting for you to come to your senses when he should be saving it for when the baby makes his official debut, and he'll actually be useful." She rubs my stomach affectionately.

"So, what I propose is...." she drags out the last word, patting my belly softly to make a muffled drum roll sound. "You come stay with me. You're not ready to move anywhere permanently, especially after the shit storm you just went through. You need time to process everything before you

make any big decisions. Specifically ones you might regret."
She looks at me pointedly.

"He'll know you're being watched over by his totally
awesome sister," she points to her chest proudly, "and that if
you go into labor I'll be able to take care of everything. He'll
also get daily updates, which will put him at ease while still
giving you the space you want right now." She nods
triumphantly as though I've already agreed to her insane
plan.

"Come on, admit I'm a genius," she teases, nudging me
affectionately.

I giggle lightly and shake my head at her infectious
humor.

"Okay." I shrug my shoulders, grateful I won't be going
apartment shopping quite yet.

I barely get the words out before Breezy is squealing and
throwing her arms around me, bouncing up and down on
her knees excitedly.

Apparently, I'm moving in with Bree.

I'm totally going to regret this.

CHAPTER TWENTY-NINE

LIV

Things move pretty quickly after deciding to move in with Breezy. I still haven't decided whether it's temporary or not, but she's been very welcoming and has left the invitation open for as long as I need.

She's pretty quickly becoming my best friend.

I found a doctor relatively easy. Dr. Fellows highly recommended her. Her name is Dr. Sarah Jolly, and we get along great. She reminds me of Wonder Woman, with long dark hair and legs that go on for miles. She also wears red scrubs all the time, but that may be a coincidence.

Because I'm 37 weeks along and am officially considered full-term, I've been going to my appointments weekly to check on my progress. Unfortunately, I'm only dilated to one centimeter, but Dr. Jolly says things can progress quickly, so I shouldn't get discouraged.

Doesn't she know you're not supposed to tell a pregnant woman what to do?

I've finished filling out the paperwork Susan dropped off at my hotel a week ago, and I am now on my way to her house to give it back so she can finish the process.

She's been very accommodating since Christmas, and I can tell she's carrying a lot of guilt for how everything played out.

I pull up in her driveway, trying to shake off the bitter memories that overwhelm me. Adam cheated on me in this house. Luke had been forced to come clean about Adam's cheating in this house.

I think I might be starting to hate this freaking house.

I take in a few deep breaths, trying to gain some control over my emotions. After a couple of minutes, I grab the door handle and swing the car door open, inviting in the bitter cold.

I hurry up the stairs to the front door of Adam's childhood home, the bank paperwork underneath my arm, and ring the doorbell. Susan opens it quickly while holding a worn leather notebook against her chest, and I can't help but eye it warily. It looks kind of familiar. I think Adam had something similar to it at one point, but I'm not sure. Thinking of my late husband brings a dull ache to my chest.

My heart is torn between gut-wrenching betrayal and a tender warmth when it comes to him. I have so many fond memories of Adam, and I hate the warring feelings bubbling up inside of me, battling which perception of him was real, making me question every moment we had together.

"Hello, Liv. It's good to see you," Susan greets me cautiously, acting as if I'm a scared little kitten. She knows it was her screw-up that caused all the drama a week ago, and she feels guilty for causing it.

"Hi, Susan," I reply, tiredly. I'm so sick of all the drama, combined with being pregnant, that I've thrown in the towel. I just want to move on, if only I knew how.

"Would you like to come in?" she questions, hesitantly.

"I actually need to get going, I just came to drop off this stuff," I reply, holding up the paperwork.

She nods slowly, seeming defeated as she takes the forms from my hands. The leather notebook is still tucked safely under her arm.

I turn to leave, wanting to avoid any more awkwardness, when Susan stops me.

"Wait."

I turn around slowly, my eyes flicking to the notebook that I just *know* has something to do with Adam. As I said before, it looks vaguely familiar, but I can't put my finger on why.

Susan licks her lips before handing me the journal as if it is one of her most prized possessions.

"Here. I went digging in Adam's high school boxes after Christmas because I couldn't believe a word *that boy* said, but I found something I think you need to see. I book-marked the pages that are the most important."

I take the bound pages and note how soft the worn leather is. I begin to flip through the paper and immediately recognize Adam's chicken-scratch handwriting.

I vaguely remember our English Lit teacher giving us an assignment at the beginning of our senior year. We were supposed to keep a journal or something and write in it every day for the school year. She had promised not to read the entries; she would just flip through them to make sure we met our requirements.

I'm not sure whether I want to tear it to shreds or hold it close to my heart while savoring every single word.

I swallow thickly before nodding at Susan and turning toward Bree's car; she was nice enough to let me borrow it.

Apparently, I have some reading to do. I just can't decide if I have the strength to study the worn pages or not.

Luke

I feel like I'm dying inside. And no, I'm not trying to be dramatic.

I've lost the other half of my soul. No one can survive that, right?

She isn't answering my calls. She isn't responding to my texts. Hell, I'm not even sure if she's reading them.

I can't stop thinking about her. The guilt is eating me from the inside out.

I'm so sorry.

Bree keeps reassuring me that Liv's fine. They went to the doctor again today, and she's dilated to two centimeters. She's feeling contractions but they aren't very consistent.

She could have the baby at any time, but it wouldn't be unheard of for her to go past her due date either, especially since it's her first child.

Since returning to Denver, I've read up on every possible scenario when it comes to delivering a baby, and the only thing I've learned is that there are too many possible outcomes to plan for anything in particular.

I find myself constantly on my phone reading about signs of labor, checking the weather, and looking up possible flights. I've mapped out my options between flying and driving, depending on departing time, and I've packed my bags. They're in the backseat of my car, ready to go as soon as I hear from Bree.

I'm hoping Liv will reach out to me when the time finally comes, but I'm not holding my breath. I hurt her and made her question my feelings, but I refuse to miss Little Man's birth.

Even if she doesn't want me there.

I won't let her down ever again.

I will *always* be here for her.

CHAPTER THIRTY

LIV

I've had the journal for two weeks. Two *long* weeks. It's 3:00 am, and I can't stop staring at the stupid leather binding as it peeks from behind my alarm clock on the bedside table. I swear it's taunting me.

Open my pages, Liv.

Read me, Liv. I dare you.

I glare at the notebook.

"Screw you," I answer back, angrily.

Great. I just yelled at a freaking book. I'm losing my damn mind.

Scratch that. I gotta cut back on the naughty language before Little Man arrives.

I'm losing my dang mind.

Ugh...

I squeeze my eyes shut tightly before throwing off my covers and finally giving in. Grabbing the journal roughly, I turn on the small decorative lamp sitting on the nightstand.

I open the worn cover and read the first page. A smile immediately graces my lips.

September 3-This is the stupidest assignment I've ever heard of.

September 4-I ate a sandwich today. The tomatoes were a good addition.

September 5- I'm already sick of school. Obviously, this is going to be a problem.

I shake my head, laughing quietly before flipping a little further into the book, looking for an entry that's longer than two sentences.

September 22-I asked Liv to the Homecoming Dance tonight. It's not like it came as a surprise or anything, but I'm still anxious to see if she says yes or if she finally figured out that she's way out of my league. How did I get so lucky to land her as my girlfriend? She's freaking perfect.

I bite my lower lip, my eyes beginning to sting. Obviously, I said yes and we had a blast at the dance. It was the perfect night.

Taking a deep breath in through my nose and releasing it through my mouth, I flip further into the journal, anxiety gnawing at my stomach.

After reading five more months' worth of entries, I start to see Adam's unique perspective on the most random things. Did you know he hated Thai food, but ate it anyway because I loved it?

He also loved pickles, although I never saw him eat them. Apparently, I had mentioned how I could still taste the pickles on his tongue after kissing him. Therefore, he never ate them again. I can't help but feel a little guilty about that one. He always put so much pressure on himself to be perfect, even when no one asked him to. It kind of breaks my heart.

Mostly, it's filled with random day-to-day things. The pressure he felt from his mom to be perfect. The pressure to go to college and make perfect grades. The pressure to break up with me. *Thanks a lot, Susan.*

I had known most of these things, but it's different reading them through Adam's eyes and being immersed in his perspective so fully.

March 7- Luke and I gamed all night last night. It was fun having a guy's night. We ate a shit-ton of pizza, played Call of Duty, and talked about random shit till 4 am. I'm gonna miss that bastard when he goes off to school. Sometimes he feels like the only real *family I have.*

I smile softly, remembering how close they used to be. When looking at Adam's old photo albums throughout the years, I couldn't help but notice Luke being in the majority of pictures with him. They really were like brothers.

It breaks my heart that I became a wedge between them after high school, that I tore apart their relationship without even knowing it.

I continue to scan the journal, and can almost hear Adam's smooth voice telling me each and every story. I feel closer to him now than I have in a long time. Struggling to swallow past the giant lump in my throat, I accept the truth.

I miss him. So much.

I turn the page to see one of the bookmarked pages that Susan has folded over.

April 12- I love her. I know we've been saying it for years now, but it's true. I love her more than anything. We just got back from prom, and she took my breath away. How gay is that? I was the luckiest guy in the room, and everyone knew it except her. She doesn't see how special she is, and I'm pretty freaking grateful for that, 'cuz if she did, I don't think she'd look my way ever again.

A tear silently slides down my cheek as I re-read this journal entry more times than I can count.

Adam, you stupid man. You have no idea how much I loved you.

I flip to the next page.

April 15- Luke can't keep his eyes off her and it makes me want to beat the ever-loving shit out of him. He's always staring at her, but it's been getting worse lately. I hate feeling jealous of my best friend. I'm the one that got the girl, not him, so why do I feel jealous of their relationship? It's not fair, and it's beginning to eat me up inside.

They have an assignment together, and I know Liv doesn't feel the same way, but I can't handle them spending so much time together. It's like watching a train wreck. I want to look away, but I can't stop staring, waiting to see where the pieces fall.

April 20- Mom threatened to take away my inheritance if I keep dating Liv. I don't know what her problem is, but it's getting ridiculous. I love Liv, but I was planning on using that money for school. I don't know what to do. Maybe she's better off without me anyway....

I shake my head, the tears falling freely now.

May 15- This is my last entry. Our assignment is due tomorrow so I won't need to write in this journal anymore. It's probably for the best; it was a pretty pointless assignment. I still haven't decided what I'm going to do about Liv. I love her, but am I enough for her?

I let out a shaky breath, afraid to read the final page.

June 2-I lied. Apparently, journal writing is a hard habit to quit cold turkey. My assignment is over, I got an A by the way, but I can't help but write one more time. Maybe by confessing my sins on to these pages it will help relieve the guilt that's eating me alive.

I made a mistake. A big freaking mistake. The worst mistake I could ever possibly make, and I've done some really dumb shit.

I'm so torn up inside, I don't know what to do. If I could take it back I would, in a heartbeat. It meant nothing.

Luke knows. He promised he wouldn't say anything, but I said some dumb shit and wouldn't blame him if he changed his mind. I'm just waiting for him to throw our friendship under the bus and sweep in on his white horse, saving the day and promising to love her forever. I should let him. It's what I deserve. It's what she *deserves.*

I've been physically ill for the past week. Literally. And she's noticed. She's been perfect, taking care of me, watching movies, bringing me soup. It only makes me want to puke more.

I can't tell her. I can't lose her. My mistake only confirmed my true feelings. How's that for irony? I would die without her. Is it selfish to keep her even though I know I don't deserve her?

Of course, it is.

I should just hand her over to Luke in a gift basket. I know I should, but I'm a selfish prick who can't let her go. I will spend the rest of my life trying to make it up to her, she just can't know. She can never find out. I want to apologize, beg her forgiveness, but I know I'll never deserve it. Go figure. I was so worried about her loyalty that I stabbed her in the back for it.

I love you, Liv.

I sit up quickly, stumbling into the bathroom and vomiting into the toilet.

The sobs begin to pour out of me, taking my breath away. As the tears stream down my cheeks, I replay everything I read just a few short minutes ago.

The guilt was eating him alive. He regretted it more than anything else in the world. It solidified his feelings for me, as weird as that sounds. He loved me, he just made the worst mistake a boy can make.

And he was a *boy* when it happened. He didn't know

how to handle all the pressure he was receiving from everyone around him.

If I had found out in high school, would I have forgiven him?

Probably not.

But I can't help but relive every tender memory he and I shared throughout our marriage, my heart aching at having possibly missed those precious moments if he'd have told me.

Can I forgive him for his mistake?

I'm not sure, but I think I need to try.

CHAPTER THIRTY-ONE

LIV

I wake up to a sharp pain in my abdomen. It's not completely out of the ordinary, but peeing my pants afterwards is.

Wait.

I look down, confused.

Rolling out of bed, and needing to clean myself up, I head to the bathroom when another contraction hits, just as strong as the last one. I lean against the doorjamb, waiting for it to pass. I breathe deeply in through the nose, out through the mouth.

After thirty seconds or so, I make it to the bathroom, more pee gushing. My brows furrow as I inspect my pajama bottoms.

"Holy shit, did your water break?" Bree yells from the doorway.

I'm sitting on the toilet with the door open, my pajama bottoms soaked. Not my best moment.

"Where the hell did you come from?" I screech, my eyes popping out of my head.

"I was on the couch watching Netflix when I heard you

coming down the hall. I then see a giant puddle on the carpet. I had assumed you were potty trained, until BAM!" She slaps her hands together loudly. "I figured out your freaking water just broke! You're paying to clean my carpet by the way," she adds, jokingly, her hands on her hips.

Before I can think of a snarky reply, another contraction hits. I remain on the toilet, attempting to breathe through the pain as Bree realizes it's not the time for teasing and runs out of the room, yelling over her shoulder, "I gotta call Luke! He's gonna kill me if he misses this!"

He's already missing this, I think to myself, instantly feeling guilty at my stubbornness, especially after reading Adam's journal.

I look around the room in a daze, wondering if I'm dreaming or not.

This can't be happening. I chant the words in my head over and over, unable to believe that I'm having a baby, and that I was stupid enough to think I could do it without Luke.

But am I too prideful to admit that to him?

Maybe.

Bree rushes into the bathroom like a chicken with its head cut off, just as I fling my soiled pajamas into the bathtub and shove the nearest hand towel between my legs, soaking up a bit more water.

Fan-damn-tastic.

Her face turns pale as she takes in my odd position. First, I'm kind of naked from the waist down. We're close and all, but not *that* close. Second, I'm hunched over, attempting to breathe through another contraction while sitting on the toilet. I'm sure I'll find this moment hysterical once the pain goes away, but as of right now, I'm kind of freaking out.

"Okay. Okay. Okay. What do I do now? I've never been a

midwife before, obviously. Although I have seen plenty of *Grey's Anatomy*, but I'm not sure the show applies in this situation. Wait, I'm not going to have to deliver the baby, right? I mean, we have plenty of time to get to the hospital. Plus, Luke will *kill* me if he misses the little guy's birth," she mumbles to herself, bouncing up and down, not knowing what to do with her nervous energy.

My contraction eases up, and I slowly sit up from my hunched position.

"You're not going to have to deliver the baby," I chuckle. "But, maybe some clothes would be nice? Dark sweats? And a few towels for the car?" I politely request.

Labor's not too bad when you're not in the middle of a contraction. *Piece of cake.*

"Yup. You got it, Livvy Lou," Bree states anxiously, giving me the thumbs up sign as she exits the bathroom.

I patiently wait for her, refusing to get the carpet any dirtier until I have some new pants on.

She places a pair of Luke's old sweatpants on the counter, along with an extra long maxi-pad and some old lady underwear. I raise my eyebrows in her direction, silently asking where she got all this stuff. She just shrugs and says, "Luke sent a care package a couple weeks ago. Who knew it would come in handy?"

A small smile graces my lips before quickly being replaced with a grimace as I breathe through another contraction.

Holy crap, that hurts.

We slip on my change of clothes, Bree grabs my hospital bag, and we slowly make our way to the car.

I'm having a freaking baby.

CHAPTER THIRTY-TWO

LIV

The ride to the hospital is rather uneventful, other than the contractions every two minutes.

Very exciting stuff.

The nurse checks us in, hooks me up to an IV, and assesses my progress. Apparently, I'm 5 centimeters dilated and should have the baby within the next few hours.

As I lay in my hospital bed, I try to ignore the overwhelming anxiety sitting in the pit of my stomach. Unfortunately, I'm too prideful to admit why.

"Do you want me to give you an update on my dear brother and his approximate whereabouts?" Breezy asks innocently. She's sitting in one of the chairs by my bed, her feet propped up as she flips through a parenting magazine. Apparently, the reading selection is scarce.

I glare in her direction, chewing my lower lip before finally deciding to swallow my pride.

"Maybe," I answer grudgingly, feeling another contraction coming.

After witnessing the contractions for the past couple of hours, Bree's anxiety has disappeared. Instead, she patiently waits for my contraction to pass before continuing. It kind of makes me want to punch her in the face.

She grins wickedly before closing the magazine and leaning her elbows on the hospital bed.

"He should be here within three hours. My parents are picking him up from the airport and driving him straight here. Can you keep your legs crossed for that long?"

I take a deep breath, grateful the pain has eased, and nod my head slightly. Three more hours. I can make it three more hours.

"What if he doesn't make it?" I whisper, voicing my greatest fear.

Why the hell did I push him away?

"He's going to make it, Liv." Bree squeezes my hand, reassuringly.

I increase the pressure, crushing Bree's fingers with my own as another contraction hits. Thankfully, my anesthesiologist should be here any minute to give me an epidural.

These women who have babies naturally are crazy. Brave. But crazy.

Bring on the drugs!

We continue to painfully pass the time for another thirty minutes before the doctor officially arrives and gives me the epidural.

I'd like to say I was able to get some rest afterwards, but nurses continue to make the rounds every thirty minutes or so, checking my progress and taking my vital signs.

I'm about ready to pass out from exhaustion when Bree steps out of the room without an explanation, quietly closing the door behind her.

She's definitely stepped up to the plate the last few weeks, and I'm extremely grateful she's here with me. I don't know what I'd do without her.

Who knew that having a baby would bring two people closer together? Ha.

A nurse comes into my room while Bree is away and checks me again.

"Looks like the baby's ready!" Nurse Cindy says, excitedly. She's an older, cheerful woman with short, white-blonde hair, and she kind of reminds me of Mrs. Claus. She even has the sparkly eyes and rosy cheeks.

I'd find her enthusiasm endearing if it weren't for my overwhelming anxiety eating a hole through my stomach.

Where the hell is Bree?

And where the hell is Luke? Three hours, my ass! I mean, butt!

I know, I know. I'm singing a different tune now that I'm in labor. Independence is not all it's cracked up to be. Apparently, I'm not big and tough like I thought I was.

"I'll go get Dr. Jolly, and we'll start pushing." She smiles kindly and heads out the door, exiting quietly.

I think I'm going to hyperventilate. Not because of the pain, modern medicine is the best thing ever, but because Bree disappeared right when I need her, and I haven't heard from Luke, either.

I may have left my phone at Bree's house, but it's not like he doesn't have her number! He could've asked her to pass along a message or something! Anything!

My breathing turns shallow as I take short little breaths in and out, forgetting everything I've learned in my Lamaze classes.

What do they know anyway?

Feeling light-headed, I try to remind myself that I can't push if I pass out. I start to sit up, trying to focus on taking deep, slow breaths.

There's a quiet knock on the door and it slowly swings

open. I hold my breath, praying for a miracle that Luke made it, when Dr. Jolly's head comes into view.

Dammit. I mean dang it!

"Hey, Liv! Ready to have this baby?" she asks, a wide smile etched into her cheeks.

I nod hesitantly while cursing Bree in my head.

Nurse Cindy joins immediately after, buzzing around the room like a busy little bee, preparing everything for Little Man to make his debut into the world.

I can't keep my eyes off the door, anxiously waiting for Bree to come back so I don't have to go through this alone.

Dr. Jolly gets into position. "Alright, Liv. We're going to wait for the next contraction, and then you're going to push nice and long, okay?"

I still haven't said a word, my eyes bouncing between Nurse Cindy, Dr. Jolly, and the entrance to my room.

My palms are sweaty as I grip my legs, feeling the pressure build.

I squeeze my eyes shut and push my heart out; Nurse Cindy counts to ten slowly, but when she reaches "five", the door swings open, banging against the wall. My eyes dart over to find a very disheveled Luke in a rumpled white t-shirt that hugs his delicious chest, a black North Face jacket, and well-worn jeans.

He anxiously scans the room before spotting me on the hospital bed. As soon as he confirms he's in the right spot, he rushes over to my side, gripping my hand tightly, and brushing his lips across my forehead.

"I know you might be mad at me, and I know you wanted to do this alone, but I just can't let you. Please don't make me miss this little guy's birth," he pleads, his eyes shining with sincerity, his hand resting on my contracting stomach.

I must be in shock because I can't seem to find my voice. Instead, I catch myself staring at Luke's scruffy cheeks, wondering if he's really here, or if I need to pinch myself.

Dr. Jolly assesses the situation, not having met Luke before. She stares at me pointedly, her eyebrows raised, while silently asking if I'm okay with him being in the room or if she needs to get security. I nod slightly, a small smile gracing my lips, finally feeling at peace. Like I *might* be able to have this baby now.

Dr. Jolly pauses for a moment before grinning cheerfully, "Alrighty, then. Let's try this again."

CHAPTER THIRTY-THREE

LIV

Twenty minutes later, I'm holding a precious baby boy in my arms. He was 7 pounds and 11 ounces, with dark peach fuzz covering his head and his daddy's pouty lips.

Luke insists he has my gray eyes.

I'm both physically and mentally exhausted, but I've never been happier or more at peace in my entire life.

Bree had apparently left to help get Luke past security, and had assumed I'd want to be alone with her brother. She wasn't wrong.

We haven't had much time to talk yet, although there's a lot that still needs to be said. For now, however, I'm just enjoying the comfortable silence encompassing the quiet room. Who knows how long it will last with all the nurses coming in to check on everything.

Luke somehow managed to squeeze his large frame into the tiny hospital bed with me and the baby, and is gazing affectionately at my Little Man while softly rubbing his fingers through my sweaty hair.

I swallow thickly, overwhelmed by the gratitude I'm

feeling for my baby, Luke, and Adam for giving me this one final gift before he left. Without him, I wouldn't have anything.

A tear silently slides down my cheek before Luke gently tilts my head toward him.

"Hey, Sweetheart," he whispers, his husky voice causing goosebumps to break across my skin.

"Hi," I whisper shyly.

He chuckles under his breath before placing a soft kiss on my forehead.

"Why so shy now, Liv?"

I shrug my shoulders. "I dunno? I'm embarrassed, I guess. I'm so sorry I left. I just needed some time to wrap my head around everything, but I'm afraid I ruined things with you. Please tell me I haven't."

He shakes his head slowly, his gaze penetrating my own. "Sweetheart, I'm afraid you can't get rid of me, no matter how hard you try. The only reason I left was to give you space. Bree convinced me it was what was best for you, and I can't tell you how sorry I am that I almost missed this little guy's birth. I would've never forgiven myself." He runs his finger along my baby's cheek softly, before turning his bright green eyes toward me.

"And I'm sorry I didn't tell you about Adam. I know I should've, and I know you think it was me choosing him over you, but it wasn't. I was an idiot and didn't know what to do. I didn't handle the situation well, but please don't let my mistake all those years ago affect our future together," he pleads.

"Can you ever forgive me?" he asks, sincerely. "I promise I will spend the rest of my life making it up to you, if you'll let me. I love you Liv. I've loved you since the first time I saw you in that stupid classroom. I loved you on prom night when I kicked myself for not fighting with Adam and letting him ask you instead. I loved you when I sat outside that chapel on your wedding day, begging you to say 'no', but wanting your happiness more than I wanted my own. I love you more than anything in the world, and I love this little guy as if he were my own, too."

I smile softly, my eyes glassy as I take in this handsome man beside me. He has no idea that I've already forgiven him, that I can't live without him, that I need him as much as he needs me.

"I love you, too," I say, simply. Honestly.

I grab the collar of his white t-shirt and pull him down for a kiss, pressing my lips to his. He pulls away slightly, a giant grin on his face, and asks, "So is that a yes?"

I nod my head and laugh before kissing him again, this time forcing all my frustration from being away from him for the past few weeks, and all my pent-up passion, into the kiss. He groans into my mouth before pulling away, and brushing my hair behind my ear, trying to calm his breathing.

Apparently, I'm not the only one with raging hormones.

"We should probably keep things G-rated for the next six weeks," he teases, bouncing his eyebrows up and down suggestively.

I laugh good-naturedly before nodding in agreement. "You're probably right."

"Besides, we have much more important things to discuss," Luke states, becoming serious.

"Like what?"

"Like this little guy's middle name, of course! Did you think I'd forget our bet?" he smirks, mischievously. "Time to pay up, Buttercup!"

Dammit. I mean, dang it! Shit this is hard. Shoot!

I had hoped he'd forgotten.

Groaning, I squeeze my eyes shut and ask the question I don't want the answer to. "And what's his middle name going to be?"

I peek at Luke, waiting for him to victoriously shout, "Danger," but am only greeted with silence.

His grin widens as he shakes his head. "Nope. Not until you tell me his first name, Sweetheart. I want to make sure it has a nice ring to it." He winks.

I glance down at my baby boy, taking in all his tiny, handsome features.

Naming kids is hard as hell. *Heck*! They're stuck with the name you choose forever, and I want to make sure it suits him perfectly.

Clearing my throat, I consider my options. "I think I've decided on...."

Luke interrupts me. "May I make a suggestion?" he asks, hesitantly.

I furrow my brows before answering, "I'll allow it."

"Well, I had been saving this for his middle name, but after seeing Little Man, I kind of think it might fit him as a first name." He looks at me a little sheepishly.

"We are not naming him Danger!" I shriek.

He chuckles before continuing, "That's not what I meant, Liv. I won't be offended if you say no, because I know he's not mine or anything," he rushes on, "but I was kind of thinking Leo, after Adam. I know he hated his middle name, Leonard, and who could blame him, that's a horrible name, but he kind of reminds me of a Leo." Luke gazes down at Little Man.

"You know, like a lion. Strong. Brave. Ready to take on the world. Plus, let's be honest, he's pretty much going to rule the house like a little king, right?" he jokes affection-ately, while rubbing Little Man's peach fuzz.

I consider his suggestion before smiling broadly. "I think that's a brilliant idea. Especially since I was going to go with Graham, after a man that I hope is going to play a pretty big part in his life." I peek up at him from beneath my eyelashes, my cheeks tinged pink, praying I didn't just make a really wrong assumption.

Luke looks at me questioningly. "Lucas Graham Jensen, and Adam Leonard Thorne?" He pauses, absorbing Little Man's name fully. "So this little guy will be Leo Graham Thorne?" He taps his chin thoughtfully. "I like it! What do you think, Liv?"

I nod my head enthusiastically, loving my decision, and ridiculously grateful Leo's middle name won't be Danger.

Hallelujah!

CHAPTER THIRTY-FOUR

LIV

W e're home. And when I mean home, I mean Luke's place back in Colorado. The drive took almost twice as long with Leo in the back, but we made it.

Luke and I both decided that we wanted to try a real relationship, and that we wanted to try it in Denver together.

Poor Luke. After flying home, driving back to Salt Lake, and then turning right back around to bring us home, he's exhausted. And I can't blame him.

He helps me carry in all of our luggage, then heads to his bathroom to shower.

I walk into the family room, smiling as I take in the familiar surroundings. I missed this place. I was only away for a few weeks, but it felt like years. Especially because I didn't know if I'd ever come back or not.

I make my way back to my old bedroom, holding Leo in one arm, my other hand lingering on the door handle as I gently push it open. My breath is immediately stolen from my lungs as I take in the freshly painted gray walls and darkly stained crib set up in the corner. My bed and dresser are missing and have been replaced with a rocking chair, changing table, and matching dresser.

My eyes glaze over as I see the giant boxes of diapers and wipes in the corner, along with a few new baby outfits hanging in the closet.

"*The Liv Whisperer* strikes again," I whisper to myself, shocked at the lengths Luke will go to make me happy, as well as the giant leap of faith he took when he rearranged his condo without knowing if I'd ever come back or not.

I collapse into the comfortable rocking chair, holding Leo close to my chest. I silently thank Adam for giving me my baby boy and for helping me find my way back to Luke. I still miss him like crazy, and will never be okay that he lied to me, but I'm learning to look at all the positive aspects of our life together instead of focusing on the shoulda, woulda, coulda.

I begin to hum a lullaby to my sweet baby boy as the sun sets through the window, painting the room in a soft orange glow.

After a few minutes, I feel eyes on me from across the room. I glance at the door to see a very handsome Luke leaning against the doorframe. He's changed into sweat pants that hang low on his hips, giving me a glimpse of his tan skin between the waistband and his t-shirt, and his hair is still damp from his shower. His eyes are full of love and affection as he takes in the scene in front of him.

I smile fondly in return before whispering, "Apparently, my room had a makeover while I was away."

He smirks at me before pushing off the frame and sauntering toward us. "I figured you'd prefer me as a roommate over Leo. You know how babies are smelly and cry a lot," he teases playfully and gently pulls me up into his arms, Leo sandwiched between us. "Unless you're too chicken to share a room with me?" he smirks.

I giggle before pulling him down for a kiss. "Not a chance."

EPILOGUE

Three Years Later

"Leo Graham Jensen! Get your cute butt down here and put your shoes on!" I yell up the staircase.

My legs are way too exhausted to make the trip up there to grab Leo, especially with my very pregnant stomach in the way.

Have *you* tried carrying a toddler while being six months pregnant? Not an easy feat.

Luke and I got married shortly after Leo was born and decided to move back to Utah in order to be closer to family. We found a cute little two-story home that has four bedrooms, and we love it. Luke is convinced we need to fill all of them with more children as quickly as possible, and I'm happy to announce we'll be having a baby girl in three *long* months.

Luke has made a point of telling Leo stories of Adam every night before bed, and it's one of my favorite traditions. The stories usually involve breaking rules of some sort, but Leo and I love hearing them.

Luke officially adopted Leo the same day of our wedding in case anything ever happened to me. He's Leo's daddy in every sense of the word and loves him as if Leo were his own flesh and blood. I'm so grateful my Little Man has two daddies he can look up to.

Speaking of flesh and blood, Susan finally learned to accept that her son wasn't perfect, but that didn't make him a bad man. She has also learned to accept Luke as her adopted son-in-law.

It's taken a lot of work, but their relationship is finally in a good place, and we can all be in the same room without any anger or hostility. Who would've thought I would end up playing referee between Susan and someone else? Adam would've loved witnessing that.

She's an amazing grandmother though, and spoils Leo like crazy while still respecting the boundaries Luke and I have set. It's been great having her close by to attend soccer games and Sunday dinners.

Luke's family also accepted Leo without batting an eye. Breezy says she always knew we'd end up together; we just had to get our heads out of our asses. *I mean butts.* They treat him like their own grandson and love him to pieces.

I gaze at the picture in the hallway as I wait for Leo to stumble down the stairs. It's a picture of Luke, Adam, and me at our high school graduation. Adam's arms are dangling around our necks, and a giant smile is plastered on his face.

I couldn't ask for a more blessed life, and I know Adam is smiling down on what we've made of it.

The End

DEAR READER

I want to thank you guys from the bottom of my heart for taking a chance on a total newbie. For giving me the opportunity to share this story with you. For rooting for the little guy. I couldn't do this without you!

I would also be very grateful if you could take the time to leave a review on goodreads or amazon. It's amazing how such a little thing like a review can be such a huge help to a new author!

ABOUT THE AUTHOR

Kelsie is a new indie author who has loved the amazing community she plunged into. Kelsie likes to spend all of her time with her three kids, an amazing husband, and two fur babies. She's addicted to sugar and goes through books like she does Ben and Jerry's ice cream! When she isn't reading or juggling kids, Kelsie can be found binging the newest television show on Netflix. If you'd like to connect with Kelsie, follow her on Facebook, sign up for her newsletter, or join Kelsie Rae's Reader Group to stay up to date on new releases, *exclusive content*, giveaways, and her crazy publishing journey.

WANT MORE?

Want to hear more about Liv and Luke?
You can find them in "Breezy" along with Bree and her steamy love interest, Derrick.
Here's an excerpt from "Breezy" by Kelsie Rae, coming June 2018.

BREEZY

"Shit," I mumble under my breath, kneeling down on to the cold laminate floor of the restaurant I'm currently working at. I always thought my brother, Luke, was full of crap when he made fun of my clumsiness, but apparently he was more on target than I gave him credit for.

I've been working at Tumblers for four months and have spilled things more times than I can count. I'm pretty sure the only reason I haven't been fired yet is because said brother is friends with my manager, Scott, or Scotty Boy, as I like to call him.

That being said, I'm wondering if he should just put me out of my misery and fire my clumsy ass. But if he does that, I'll be royally screwed unless I can find another job...and fast. One that isn't in the restaurant industry, obviously. And if the past six months have taught me anything, it's that jobs are freaking hard to come by!

Let me rephrase that: Jobs in my graduating profession, when you don't have previous experience, are hard to come by.

I graduated about six months ago with a Human Resources degree, which is fan-freaking-tastic, but have had no luck finding a job. They all want previous experience, which is impossible to have if no one will hire you in the first place! It's one of those, what came first, the chicken or the egg scenarios. I need the experience to get a job, but I need a job to get the experience.

Hence, my current kneeling position, cleaning up nachos with diet coke splashed all over my white blouse.

Well, it *was* white.

I'm sure I'll be laughing about this tomorrow, but right now I just want to punch the asshole who bumped into me, causing me to spill nachos all over myself and the stranger in booth 14.

"I am so sorry!" I apologize, scraping melted cheese off a pair of expensive-looking black loafers. I'm currently scrambling underneath the table, practically giving the guy a shoe shine, and feeling a bit too guilty to stand up and face the victim whose shoes I just ruined.

Well, I didn't ruin them. But I'm going to have to take the fall for it anyway.

Dammit. I'm totally losing my job. At least I have an interview tomorrow, right?

I attempt to clean the mess with my dirty rag and hear chuckling near my bent position on the floor.

Looking up, I'm met with a pair of gorgeous icy blue eyes glinting at my compromising position, his smug face mere inches from my own.

He's laughing at me!

I feel a blush creep into my cheeks before clearing my throat and crawling out from underneath the table.

I clench my fists at my sides, about to defend my clumsiness even though it wasn't really my fault, when the stranger in front of me lifts his hands in mock surrender, his eyebrows practically reaching his hairline.

Apparently, he's good at reading body language. Or maybe he can feel the anger radiating off me in waves. Regardless, I can feel his eyes scanning me from head to toe, taking in my dark curly hair piled on top of my head, along with my still-soaked white blouse and black pencil skirt that likes to hug my curvy hips.

I'm an absolute mess, and I don't exactly appreciate him making that assessment.

Taking in a deep breath through my nose, I remind myself that he is not the enemy. The jackass who bumped into me is, and if I want to keep my job then I need to play nice with the customers.

Even the condescending ones.

I refuse to acknowledge that Nacho Guy is ridiculously handsome and absolutely huge. He reminds me of a Viking warrior with a broad chest, tapered waist, and muscular thighs that also seem to be covered in ground beef and tortilla chips.

Oops.

I bite my lip. I'm feeling a little guilty as I assess the damage of the poor guy's stained pants before making my way back to his face and taking in his crystal blue eyes once more, along with messy blonde hair, stubble covered cheeks, and lickable tan skin.

I squeeze my eyes shut, feeling my cheeks heat all over again.

Lickable, Breezy? Really?

I peek one eye open and find myself staring at Nacho Guy's frosty eyes for a third time, a smirk plastered on his stupidly handsome face. And I just spotted a dimple in his left cheek.

Dammit!

I'm a sucker for dimples.

I swallow my pride; it's bitter taste lingering in my dry mouth. "I'm sorry about your pants and shoes." I motion awkwardly toward his lower half, causing Nacho Guy to look down at his soiled clothes.

His deep chuckle makes another appearance before he shrugs his broad shoulders and reaches forward to shake my hand. "Not the first time I've been covered with cheese. Won't be the last. I'm Derrick."

I place my hand in his warm palm; it's heat causing my insides to melt just like the cheddar on his pants. He shakes my hand once before releasing it. "Not the first time?" I tease, placing my hands on my hips with my eyebrows raised. "Do you often make a habit of spilling food in your lap?"

He laughs again, shaking his head back and forth before replying. His voice is a bit of a gruff baritone that causes me to shiver slightly. "Technically, I'm not the one that spilled the cheese," he looks at my nametag, "Rylee. But yes, my nieces and nephew have made a mess of my clothes a time or two."

I'm confused as to why he called me the wrong name then peek at my nametag. It does, in fact, read "Rylee." I must have grabbed the wrong one in the breakroom, but I decide not to correct Nacho Guy. I mean Derrick. My lack of attention to detail might have just saved my job. A mischievous smirk graces my lips before I quickly hide it behind my hand, faking a light cough.

"Ah, yes. Those blasted nieces and nephews. How dare

your siblings procreate!" I flirt, shaking my fist in the air in frustration and causing his deep chuckle to reverberate.

"They're the worst!" Derrick agrees passionately, though I can tell he's teasing. "Do you have any nieces or nephews?"

I hesitate before answering. I'm wondering if I should answer as fake Rylee, or real Bree, when I finally decide to give him an honest answer.

"Yeah, actually. My brother had a baby boy a little while ago. I think he's like six months or so? Technically, it's not his baby, but it's complicated. Either way, he's my adopted nephew, and is the absolute cutest thing on the planet. And you're right about the messes during dinnertime. That kid's a disaster!" I smirk in Derrick's direction.

"I don't even mind cleaning up after meals. The worst part is that as soon as they start eating real food, their poop starts to reek!" he laughs.

My nose wrinkles at his apt description, knowing he's not wrong. Last time I babysat Leo, I debated on searching for a gas mask or just hosing him off in the backyard. The smell was *that* bad.

"Yeah, I don't envy whoever's on diaper duty in their household," I joke, noticing a couple at a nearby table trying to grab my attention.

Rylee is definitely going to get fired by the end of the night if I don't get my butt in gear.

"Well, let me bring you an appetizer or something for your trouble. I'm really sorry about the mess." I start to make my way to the other table, but Derrick's gruff voice stops me.

"Don't worry about it Rylee. I don't think I'd mind cleaning up your messes." I glance over my shoulder at his offhand comment, surprised to see his baby blue eyes still fixed on me, and a flirtatious grin plastered on his kissable lips as he continues to ignore the other two gentlemen at his table.

I quirk my eyebrow and give him my signature smirk before turning toward the other table, effectively ending our conversation. Even so, it stays on constant replay through my mind for the rest of the night.